A PLAGUE OF GODS

A PLAGUE OF GODS

Nine Stories and an Epic Poem

CATHERINE LANDIS

CLH

Cover design by Bruce Henschen, Sr.

For my sons,

Bruce, Jr., and Charlie

CONTENTS

Medusa   3

Atalanta   19

Ariadne   32

Arachne   40

Echo   50

Callisto   69

Phaethon & Aescalpius   76

Baucis   87

Icarus   98

Gilgamesh   102

❁ ❁ ❁

Introduction

Herein are nine stories and an epic poem.

The stories are based loosely on a selection of Greek or Roman myths, and all are set in 2020 or early 2021 during the first months of the global pandemic of SARS CoV-2 when life, as we thought we knew it, changed in ways that felt fantastical and unforeseen. For me, those early months recall a kind of innocence, tinged with death and reports of death, but also of hope, like a rebirth, as if we might be running through some sort of fire, but we would come out on the other side, unscathed. Pretty much. Any day now...

Even the stubbornest of mythologies can be eclipsed by reality.

These stories are not retellings of the old myths, rather, each story contains an essence of the original, a seed embedded, to offer a mythic framework for this profoundly strange and anxious time. With one exception, they are told from the point of view of women who, in the original myths, were reduced to the roles of goddesses, monsters, or beautiful maidens. The women in these stories defy reduction, and they have a thing or two to say about these times.

The poem is a modern interpretation of *The Epic of Gilgamesh*, also from the point of view of two women. The original *Gilgamesh* is a long poetic composition about a young, partly-divine, king of a Sumerian city-state who learns that he must shed childish delusion and wishful thinking if he hopes to grow up. It is a hero's tale, a journey, begun in grief and madness, to hunt down the nature of death.

I had felt compelled to write a modern-day version of *The Epic of Gilgamesh* for a very long time. For decades it haunted me. Never have I found a story that so precisely encapsulates the only way my life makes sense to me: because I will die, how shall I live? But every time I sat down to write, I ran into a dead end. If you're going to reinvent an epic, you'd better have a good reason, and never could I find one worthy of the original. Then came COVID-19.

A global pandemic screams for a new story of an old story about death.

Medusa

Medusa was a Gorgon with hair of hissing serpents. Her glance could turn a person into stone. Perseus was the son of Jupiter, King of the Gods, and of Danea, a beautiful woman, naturally. Her father had been told that he would be killed if Danea ever had a son, and so he locked mom and baby in a wooden chest and set them afloat on the sea. They were picked up on land ruled by Polydectes. When Perseus grew up, it was Polydectes who sent him on the quest to bring him the head of Medusa. Perseus succeeds, but only with the help of some sea nymphs and the Messenger God Mercury. In other words, magic. A helmet that made him invisible, a pair of winged sandals, a shield, and a pouch for Medusa's head.

"I'm not getting my goddamn nose fixed." Medusa stood up. She walked to the edge of the porch.

Her sisters looked at each other. Cecilia shook her head, leaned back in the chair, closed her eyes. Frances leaned forward. Elbows on knees, she looked down at her feet. "We're just trying to help," she said.

"It's my face," Medusa said.

"I know it," Frances said.

"We were just thinking it might be a good time," Cecilia said.

"We're in freaking quarantine, Meddy," said Frances. "Like, what else are you doing?"

"By the time all this is over, nobody will remember what you used to look like," Cecilia said.

"That's all we're saying," Frances said.

"People will just think, wow, doesn't Medusa look great! But they won't know why. They won't know what's different," Cecilia said.

"Clean slate," Frances said.

Medusa was not responding to the clean slate idea. She was not responding. Which caused her sisters to turn again to each other. What now?

Cecelia tried a different angle. "*Of course* you didn't want to do it when it was Mom's idea, but Mom's not here anymore. This time you'd be doing it for you. Nobody else. It might give you more confidence."

Medusa turned around. She smiled at her sisters. She said, "What could you possibly mean by more confidence?"

Cecilia sighed.

Frances put her head in her hands.

Medusa drew an imaginary circle in front of her face with the index finger of her right hand. Around once, then around again. She said, "See my face? This is my face. This is my face saying, I don't give a shit." She turned back around, placed her hands on the railing, and looked out at the yard.

It wasn't her yard. But the man who rented the place to her said she could do what she wanted with it, and so she'd torn out the fescue and planted varying crops of switchgrass, Indian grass, hairgrass, and blue gamma, separated by snaking paths of field stones. These grasses, they never needed mowing and from the porch, it was like looking out at a tall grass sea undulating in shades from green to pink to variations on tan and brown. Beyond the grasses, the trees were greening up and the wildflowers were in bloom along the narrow road and in the vacant lot across the road. It was a reason to live in Georgia, this budding, this blooming, this color, this spring. Medusa used it to defend her decision to live in a place that did not seem to want her. You put up with a little winter, but then, look what you get! Today the sky was clear enough to see the mountains to the north, partially obscured by a low band of thin clouds under a pale blue sky. These days she had to remind herself to remember what she had, not what she had lost, even though the world felt drenched in loss, and the air charged with dread. She felt charged, her skin tingly, breath shallow, muscles tensed in anticipation of ... what? That was the problem. No one seemed to know what. The very ends of her hair felt electric.

But the sky was blue and the mountains were visible and the trees were budding and her sisters had driven up from Atlanta to see her. Maybe she shouldn't have snapped at them. They meant well, she knew it. They were just in a bind. How to come right out and say the obvious -- your nose is too big -- without saying, you're ugly. She was not ugly. They had been telling her that for as long as she could remember. *You're not ugly.*

But.

Always there came that *but. But are you sure you want that doughnut? But a little lipstick won't kill you. But what if you brushed your hair?*

If her nose was a tad long and her hair, (well, her hair was another story), so what? What did it mean to be not ugly? Her sisters were considered beautiful, but by whom? Who was the decider?

Their friends, yes.

Men, no kidding.

The consensus of the society they happened to live in, of course.

They were tall, thin, and relatively blonde white women. Medusa was not beautiful, but she was not ugly. She was unusual. Striking. Some people found her scary. All her sisters wanted to know was, what if she could do something about it?

Medusa didn't care. That was the answer. It was the truth. Her sisters were considerably older than she was, and it had made a difference. When she was born, Frances was 15 already, and Cecilia, 14. She was their baby, too. They had tried to shield her, as much as was possible without getting singed themselves, from their mother, who had been no less mercurial and relentlessly critical of them, but they were two, bound together. When they left home, they left Medusa, five years old, alone.

Their mother was mercurial and relentlessly critical, but she became newly enraged when her husband, their father, hung himself in a closet two months after Medusa was born. Two months. A closeted hanging. A shameful and cowardly betrayal. Medusa was blamed. Even as a child, Medusa was attributed with powers she had no idea she possessed.

Once, after their mother died, Medusa and her sisters stayed up all night drinking whiskey around the kitchen table and snort laughing over the litany of complaints. Frances was careless but also too careful, shy but also too loud, smart but never smart enough, the one who could be counted on to exhibit bad judgement and did not finish anything she started. Cecilia was rude, ungrateful, and overbearing but also unwilling to stand up for herself. She was impatient and an insufferable perfectionist. She had dreadful taste and was always late. Medusa, well, it was all about the hair and the face and the weight and that nose that must have come from some long-buried genetic cesspool, on her father's side, no doubt.

The trick was, Medusa had never cared about what she happened to look like. Her mother was a silly woman. Unlike her sisters, who wore their mother's complaints like second skins, she had no reason to listen to silly women. Medusa was born busy. She couldn't be bothered. When she was younger, she had spelling words to study and a math level to skip and then field hockey games to play, and softball and crew, and debates to win, and then came law school to get through and jobs to navigate, until she found herself with picket lines to join. It was serious business, her life. Her physical appearance was far down on the list of things she had ever cared about.

Was that allowed? Through the laughter and the alcohol, Medusa had tried to explain.

"I never cared," she said.

Cecilia stopped laughing and glanced at Frances, who poured another whiskey. Her sisters did not believe her.

But here they were, up from Atlanta to visit. So what if they did not understand her. She did not understand them! Together they had survived their father's suicide and their mother's berating, forging a bond stronger than understanding, and it was going to get old, she could tell, this living alone in a pandemic.

A car was coming up the road. That was unusual. Her house, far from the highway, on the top of a hill among more trees than neighbors, suited Medusa because most of the year she spent in hotel rooms, shuttling between cities, organizing people, bolstering them with hope she secretly did not have so much of anymore. And so, when she was home, what she wanted was to be left alone. Hardly anyone bothered to come out this far from the highway and almost no one came up the hill. But the car was coming, slower and slower now until it stopped in front of her house. A young man got out of the car and began walking up the driveway.

"Who is this asshole?" Medusa said.

It was a bit of a climb. The young man was striding. Long legs effortlessly taking the hill, occasionally looking down at a clipboard he held in his hand. On his head, a red hat.

"Where's your mask?" Medusa called out when he got close enough so she did not have to yell.

The young man stopped, dug his hand into the pocket of his khakis, came out empty. He laughed. "I must have left it in the car," he said, but then he continued walking, oblivious to the point of cutting through her tall grasses rather than circling around on the flagstone path that led to the porch steps.

"What the hell are you doing?" Medusa said. "Stop right there."

By this time Cecilia and Frances had slipped masks on their faces and joined her at the edge of the porch.

The young man slowed down but he did not stop. He took a step and then another while peering down at the clipboard as if following directions he did not understand.

With the index finger on her left hand, Medusa drew an imaginary circle in front of her face. Around once and then around again. "This is my face," she said. "Telling you not to take one more step."

The young man did not look at her face, but he did stop. The two other women on the porch were less intimidating, even though their faces were masked, or half masked. He turned and focused on them. Grinning, he said, "Just making sure you ladies are registered to vote."

Perseus was his name.

His father was a goddamn god. Which is to say, a commercial real estate developer in a place that would not quit, at a time when you could not lose. His mother was beautiful, of course. His stepfather was a problem.

His stepfather had asked him to move. "I love your mother and I love you, but we can't have this much division in this house," he had told Perseus.

His mother did not take sides. But then, she pointedly did not take his side.

"Really, Mom?" he had said, but his mother, earbuds fixed, was heading out for a run and did not appear to hear him.

His stepfather gave him until the end of the week. His stepfather was a Democrat. Also a Jew.

Perseus packed some clothes, his computer, his PS5, and the framed Beer Pong Champion certificate his KA brothers had made up for him as a joke, even though he was honored, seriously, and moved in with two guys he'd met at the gym. Two guys who had done more to open his eyes than anybody he'd ever met in school. They knew things other people did not know, the real story behind the stories, the clues to look for to protect you from turning into one more of the blind and stupid sheep walking numbly away from their own freedom. *Where are you getting your information, son*, his step-father was always asking, but his stepfather wouldn't believe the truth if it was a snake that bit him.

That was the kind of thing these guys liked to say. They used colorful language. They knew how to get in the last word. These guys were ripped, tattooed with crosses. They worked out every day. When the gym was shut down, the owner let them in the back door as long as they didn't tell anybody and kept the lights turned off. At home they drank protein shakes. Also George Dickel. They sweated and threw their sweaty shirts and shorts and socks into a pile in front of the washing machine. One day, one of them yelled, "This place smells like a pigsty!" Perseus could not smell a thing.

Within the week, all three young men had tested positive for the virus along with the owner of the gym and the girlfriend of the owner of the gym and her sister and the Cross-Fit trainer. It was kind of a cluster.

Perseus lay on the couch, chugging Gatorade, not smelling, with a runny nose and sore throat. He listened to the moans from the back bedroom where his buddy fought a fever. He ignored the comings and goings of his second roommate, who felt fine, calling his roommates pussies, and who saw no need to quarantine because those tests, who can trust them?

Perseus watched TV. On the TV, he watched the marchers. Masked marchers. They looked like monsters. Like insects. Like an unholy alien species. Especially that one. Wait. He knew her, but how?

She was a white woman in a line of mostly black women walking arm in arm down the street, so she stood out, but it was more than that. Even with a mask on, Perseus recognized her, but from where? Surely this was not one of his mother's friends. Not the mother of a friend, not a former teacher. Someone from the maid service? The women were marching straight toward the police. Marching arm in arm like a flesh-covered battering ram, like lemmings on their way toward a cliff, but this one woman, her hair like a nest of snakes, electrically charged, writhing about in the humid breeze, who was she? Perseus let out an involuntary whistle.

"That is one ugly bitch," said the roommate who felt fine.

"Antifa," said the other roommate, as he staggered out of the bedroom to see what was going on.

"Is it a man or a woman?" the first one said.

"All lives matter," the second one said.

"It ought to be a crime to be that ugly."

"She looks dangerous."

"What's up with that hair?"

"Antifa, I'm telling you."

These marchers pissed off his buddies to no end.

Round 'em up.

Smoke 'em out.

Shoot 'um up.

Then Perseus remembered. It was the hair. It was the woman with the crazy hair on the porch of the house at the top of that hill in Pickens County. He moved closer to the television for a better look. The cameras gravitated to her also, white arms in a line of black arms, but again, that hair. It was hard to see her face under the mask, but it hardly mattered. She would stand out anywhere. He caught the anger from his friends, felt the surge of it speeding up his heart, tightening his jaw. He was angry, not just because she had been mean to him, not just because the camera could not stay away from her, not just because of the message shooting from her eyes -- *you can't fuck with this* -- and not just because these people, these people, these goddamn people made him so mad he could barely see straight, but all of it.

He sought counsel from his father.

Not in person, of course. His father was a busy man, and Perseus, at the moment, was a disappointment. He had failed to get into the MBA program his father had recommended, after being tossed from the honors program for not keeping his grades up in college. He had flamed out at the job his father had gotten him, but that one wasn't his fault. (No one had told him about vacation days until *after* he'd come back from Cancun. Jesus!) Texting was safer.

By that time, there were pictures all over the internet of the woman with the wild hair marching, so these were the pictures he sent to his father, along with a version of the story of how the woman had laughed at him. Through text, it was impossible to describe that laugh, piercing, screeching, almost nonhuman, and how it had come at him so suddenly, like a gust of wind, it nearly knocked him down. And how, in an unexpected chilling stillness, had come the words the woman had said to him once she and the other two women on that porch finally stopped laughing.

Not only are we registered to vote, sweetheart, your guy is going to fucking lose so fucking hard he'll be slinking out of Washington on his fucking knees.

Hard to get all that in a text. But Perseus did his best, knowing that his father was predisposed to disapprove of the marching people and their so-called cause. When his father did not answer right away, Perseus risked adding a second text. *Honestly, I wanted to punch her face in.*

His father had a better idea.

As it happened, the woman with the snake hair lived on the top of a hill in Pickens County in a house she was renting from a man who had bigger plans. His father texted a picture of the proposed development and a map. Perseus enlarged the map and peered at it to make sure he was telling his father the right street, but his father knew the area well enough to know it hardly mattered which street. Soon the entire hill would be swallowed by a gated golf community. *We can arrange for that to happen sooner than later,* his father texted. *Either way, her lease can run out.*

You can do that?

Is that a question? Perseus's father was habitually amazed whenever anyone underestimated him.

Perseus felt the pause in his father's voice as surely as if a hand had been placed on his shoulder to signal that he should sit still, be quiet, and wait. His father was thinking.

His father was thinking; he was not opposed to giving a young man a second chance or a third or fourth. Or a fifth. Depending, of course, on the young man. At his disposal were myriad trials and tests he could throw out on the chance that his son would pass one of them, one of these days. He texted, *Somebody's got to be the one to tell her she's got to move. In the middle of a pandemic.*

I am not afraid, texted Perseus, thumbs flying, face beaming with the relieved smile of a lucky young man.

Perseus carried with him another clipboard. He wore a flag pin and a red hat. This time Medusa did not see him coming until he was almost at her door. It was a hazy morning and sweltering already. She had all the windows open for the cross breeze, reluctant to turn on the air conditioner unless she absolutely could not stand it, not because she was trying to be noble or righteous or make a point about anything, but because she liked feeling the cross breeze. And she liked hearing the immediacy of the sounds coming through the window, the birds, the cicadas, the rustling grasses. She had not expected to be this lonely.

But these days she found herself precariously close to tears. She was unused to feeling fragile and did not know how to think about what it would mean for her to lose her grip, to be one of those people searching for the ground under their feet. Doubt invaded her mind, questioning the inevitability of justice, the possibility for change, her ability to make any damn difference. It was to soften this doubt that she allowed herself small indulgences such as the intimacy with the breeze and the birds and the rustling grasses, a new linen shirt delivered through the mail, good bread and expensive cheese, wine in the evenings. There was time now for long phone conversations with old friends, but there were also times when she started to pick up the phone but then hesitated. And then, didn't call. Working from home was making her feel uneasy, as if she was missing something, as if somebody was getting away with something, as if this splintering might be worse than the risk of working together. Solidarity might starve on a diet of zoom and email.

But the emails were piling up. The unanswered felt as oppressive as the heat. She was on her laptop at her desk, sifting through them when she heard his footsteps.

There he was, on the flagstone path, the young man with a red hat and a clipboard.

"No mask, again, I see," she said, stepping onto the porch to stop him.

Perseus stared down at the clipboard. Was he nervous? Pausing for dramatic effect? It was hard to tell. Finally he slid the paperwork from the clipboard, two pages stapled at the top left corner. He did not look at her face. Instead, looking down at the porch steps in front of him, he held it out to her.

"What is this?" she said.

He started to come closer, but she stopped him. "Just put it on the step and back away, please," she said.

He backed up. Still fidgeting with the clipboard, he backed nearly into the grasses that lined the path, taller now and brown from weeks without rain. She leaned down and picked up the papers. She read through page one and page two. She said, "My lease extends through the rest of the year."

"The bulldozers will be here in October," said Perseus.

"This can't be legal."

"Go ahead and sue."

She laughed. It was that same laugh, piercing, screeching, ferociously not human, and she would not stop. Like an eruption from a bottled up well. She laughed and she kept laughing, with her snake hair flying about her head, and the longer she laughed, the smaller he felt. His mother, he knew, would not be happy with him right now. But his father. His father was a goddamn god.

Perseus wanted to do something to stop this woman from laughing. This was serious. He was serious. She should not be laughing.

He dug his hands into his pocket for the matchbook. He had picked it up the night before at the sports bar that was, defiantly, open, where he'd gone to watch the Braves play in an empty ball park that should not have been empty. She was not the only one bottled up with impotent fury, no sir. Tearing off a match, he lit it and held it up. At his feet, the tall grass was dry from too many weeks without rain. It would go up pretty fast. He calculated how fast.

Medusa on the porch, stopped laughing and also calculated.

"You would burn it down?" she asked.

"I would burn it down and leave nothing but the dirt and stones."

"You're a child."

"You're a monster."

Atalanta

Atalanta was a Boeotian maiden who could run exceptionally fast. It was prophesied that marriage would kill her. But she was beautiful, of course, and had a bunch of suiters. She set up a race, stipulating that any man who beat her could marry her, but if they lost, they died. It was a safe bet. Being such a fast runner, she beat all of them.

Venus, Goddess of Love, intervened. She helped the suitor Hippomenes by giving him three golden apples to throw around during the race to distract Atalanta, and it worked. Atlanta was distracted, and Hippomenes won.

Val is promising pie.

"I don't care what kind of pie he makes," Atalanta says, "I'm not coming."

"It's apple."

I don't care."

Wait a sec."

Atalanta hears Val on the other end of the phone walking across the floor of her kitchen, opening the door to the garage, from where the high-pitched grinding of a table saw can be heard. That would be Hippomenes at his woodworking, his new hobby. When it stops, Val calls to him, *It's apple, right?*

Back on the line with Atalanta, Val says, "Apple it is."

"Please don't ..."

Wait." Another call out to the garage. *Pie or cobbler?*

"It's pie," she tells Atalanta. "And two kinds of ice cream."

"... do this to me."

Atalanta had not imagined it would be this hard. She turns the phone to speaker and lays it on the counter and runs her fingers through her hair.

"Come on, Atty, tomorrow night, 6 o-clock, what else are you doing? It'll be just you and me and Hip and the Powell's. Jen and Mark, remember? You like them, right? And Ned."

And Ned. Of course. Ned, the latest in the string of men Val and Hippomenes have come up with for Atalanta to meet in hopes of finding her a husband. Even though she does not want a husband. She's told them, a million times. They don't believe her. Rather, Val believes that Atalanta *thinks* she doesn't want to get married, but secretly she also believes that Atalanta does not know how much happier she *could* be. And Hippomenes, who knows what he's thinking. Every once in a while, and only when Hippomenes has had one glass of whiskey too many, Atalanta gets the feeling he might like a turn in that string of men. Maybe for a night. Or a weekend here or there. Perhaps what he's thinking is that some version of a Ned, or a Dustin or a Chris or a Tommy, would blunt the temptation, since a woman taken is easier to resist than one just out there, dangling.

It could also be she's imagining things.

She would never say a word of this to Val. Of course. Atalanta stares at the phone lying on the counter and imagines Val's voice lifting out of the speaker like a smoke plume.

"Atty?"

She should say something. But already she has said, no, has she not? And that wasn't good enough.

"You want us to wear masks?" Val's voice rises from the phone, lying on the counter.

Masks? Atalanta would like to say. *Is this a question? Of course you should fucking wear masks! That you even have to ask!!! You people!!! Why on earth do you think I'm not coming?* But she won't say that. She does not know what to say to her sweet, caring, careless friend. She says, "Tell Hip to save me a piece of that pie, okay? I've got to go."

Go where?

Where did she have to go?

She had not imagined it would be this hard or last this long. What was worse, to *be* alone or to insist on being alone for no good reason? Are you a hero or a chump to follow the rules when nobody else seems to bother. The good girl scout, teacher's pet, hall monitor, camp counselor, the only grown-up in the room. Atalanta sits down at the kitchen table, which has become her office now, in front of the laptop where she had been drafting one more fundraising letter to people who are not in a mood to be handing out money in these unprecedented times. Already, she is doubting herself.

It was different when the weather was warm. In the spring, when this pandemic stuff was new, and throughout the summer and into the early fall, they could eat out on the porch, and everybody brought their own food and utensils and wine, and on display there would be a new salad bowl to admire, or a cutting board or a wooden vase that Hip would have made in his workshop in the garage. Sometimes it would just be her and their daughter Bess, although Bess tended to take her food back to her room where she gutted through her own private hell as a teenager in a pandemic. Other times there'd be another couple, and sometimes this Ned, who was as interesting as the Styrofoam cup he brought to pour his beer in. Still, it made her nervous. This virus. Who could say, really, how risky it was outside on that porch. She'd get antsy and leave early and drive home, promising herself to never do that again. Until the next time Val called.

Now the weather has turned cold, and the porch is no longer feasible, even with heaters. Val and Hip continue to include her, as always, only now it's for dinner in the dining room, and it's so damn close to getting those vaccines, and the risk is not worth it, and she always says, no, and it's hard and tiresome, and all she can think is, why does she have to be the party pooper. Nothing she does feels like the right thing to do.

She is grateful to Val and Hip for including her. She is angry at Val and Hip for being so reckless. She vacillates. It bugs her that she can't land on one way to feel. These days it's always this *and* that. It's getting harder and harder to make a decision on any damn thing. It's getting harder and harder to know her own mind. More than once she has wondered if her purpose in life might be to make everybody around her feel sane.

She is exhausted. Why are there no answers? Why won't somebody tell her what she should do? Why does she have to figure out this shit all by herself? Her mind races as if stuck on an infinity loop that lands her back where she started, with no answers. She clicks on the link to the pound to see if there are any new dogs.

Any small dogs. She has told herself she would need a small dog, but there never are many of those. Only big dogs. Pit Bull mixes, mostly. She wonders, as she has before, if she could handle a big dog. Seeing the needy eyes looking back at her from the computer screen, she tries to imagine a big dog lying on the kitchen floor next to her feet. She does not have time for a big dog or a little dog or any dog. She has no time and no money, and still she imagines calling out through her empty house, here

Lexi, here Scout, here Maggie, here Buddy. Like another
infinity loop to chase.

The next morning she is running. She is running and
still vacillating and half-listening through her earbuds
to a singer Val has been insisting Atalanta must hear. It
is a woman singing, a woman who sounds like a little
girl who slur-speaks her lyrics, the lyrics Val swears are
profound. If you could only hear them. The girl/woman's
voice sounds sad, slurring the lyrics, whatever they are.
Atalanta is half-listening because she can't stop thinking about something she remembered just this morning
while she was filling her water bottle. The memory was
disturbing enough, but worse was the fact that this thing
she remembered never happened. It could not have happened. And yet it's vivid in her mind, not like a dream,
but like a real memory. Like a real moment in a real time
and place, only which time and place?

That's the problem. She remembers she was driving
and she was alone. She remembers it was on a freeway
but where? That part she does not remember, not where
she was, or where she was driving to, or where she had
come from. A pack of cigarettes was tucked inside her
purse on the passenger seat. It was not that she had
started up smoking again, this was merely a lark, a secret
treat. Nobody had to know. Nobody did know. She would
smoke only one cigarette, and that would be it, and the
memory revolved around trying to decide when to light
up, a back and forth that went through her mind: *would*

now be a good time? What about now? All of that, the purse and the cigarettes and the back and forth, she remembers clearly, but where had she been?

Nowhere.

On a freeway.

But which freeway?

She can't remember. The location flickers outside of her consciousness as she is running. It is disturbing. Irritating. She stops the music and takes out the earbuds so she can think, but she cannot bring the flickering into focus. She remembers slipping the pack out of the purse, pulling the cigarette out of the pack, putting it into her mouth, lighting it, feeling the jolt to her lungs, opening the window and blowing smoke. She remembers the exhilaration of getting away with it. But where was that, and when?

Not in her 20's. She was 25 when she quit smoking, and it was hard, and she would have remembered relapsing. Relapsing would have been traumatic. But her 30's she spent mostly in Chicago writing two novels and four plays that never went anywhere. Would something have broken her way had she stayed longer? Who knows. It's a waste of time to wonder. She ran out of money and that was that, but one thing she does know, she never once smoked in Chicago. Also, she did not own a car.

But since coming home, there has not been any particular time when she would have been tempted to smoke, nor – and crucially -- has there been a person she might have wanted to hide it from. So what if she smoked a cigarette; who would care? Atalanta claws through the years of her life but cannot find a slot into which she can wedge this memory of driving and secret smoking. It is a memory hiccup. It's like an extra chapter slipped into the book of her life.

So it had to be a dream. A smoking dream. But smoking dreams always woke her up sweating, heart racing, and this was not like that. It was not like any dream she'd ever had. It was more like a puzzle. Like a mystery. Like there was a moment in her past when her life divided into two lives, and she has been living one life, while the other Atalanta has been living a different life on another plane of existence where, on at least one day, that other Atalanta smoked a cigarette on a lark in her car on a freeway. Something must have happened to crack open the two planes of existence long enough to glimpse the other side, and now the boundary is blurred and she carries the memories of two Atalantas.

Which is crazy. She does not want to think she's going crazy.

She is running 12 miles today, and at the six mile mark, she slows to a walk and turns around. In Chicago she got used to running alongside Lakeshore Drive in the mornings before breakfast, except winters when the path iced over, and she would have to wait until the thaw. Nothing ever ices over down here and, frankly, it's easier to run no matter what the season, but somehow she lost the running habit. Hip had found her a job at the theater where he was on the board of directors.

Not writing plays, goodness no, but press releases and fundraising letters and social media posts. Running had been the thing that got her going in Chicago when she spent her days alone, writing, but she was in marketing now. She was a marketer. She was not, in fact, running at all when the pandemic hit. She had pretty much abandoned it for spin classes, yoga, and whatnot. For fuck-it, meeting friends at the Public House, drinking canned wine, and talking about tedious men and poorly written books by people who managed to get published anyway.

But this pandemic was something else! The office went remote. The theater shut down. The gym closed. The yoga studio closed. The Public House closed. Events got postponed. Events got cancelled. Days went by when Atalanta wasn't seeing one human being except on a computer screen. March turned to April turned to May. How long would this last? There were rumblings of a year or more, but there was something fantastical about that amount of time. Fantastical to the point of impossible. In May she pulled her running shoes from the back of her closet and ran two miles. Then she ran three. In June she ordered new shoes and ran four. By July she was running six, three days a week and then four days, and feeling lucky to have something to look forward to. In September when she ran nine miles she knew she was not going to stop. Friends began to weigh in.

"You're going to hurt your knees," one said.

No, I'm not, she would think.

"You're going to ruin your feet," said another.

No, I'm not.

"Are you eating enough protein?"

Why do you care?

Naturally Val and Hip had their say. Atalanta understood that Val would feel as if she had a stake since she was the one who got her into running in the first place. All those years ago. They were 25. In college they had played a little intramural soccer and some midnight racquet ball, but nothing that required undue exertion. Val had started running to keep her mother from driving her crazy over the wedding arrangements, and Atalanta was trying to convince her that she and Hip really didn't want to just go down to the courthouse and be done with it. It had been a particularly awkward moment. Atalanta trying to talk Val back into a real church wedding with the flowers and the cake and the band and the first dance and the tossing of the bouquet, when both of them knew that Atalanta would have preferred to be talking Val out of getting married in the first place. But weren't these the bones of friendship? Knowing each other's minds without the need to say the words? Driving to the florist, a silence swollen with words unsaid.

Atalanta lit a cigarette, cracked open the window, and blew out the smoke. "A wedding will be fun," she had said, finally.

"How about you put down that damn cigarette and come running with me?" Val had said.

Okay.

It wasn't as easy as all that, but it worked. They ran, Val got married, and Atalanta quit smoking and moved to Chicago. Now Val was offering to run with her again. Practically begging. "Let me know if you want me to join you," she would say.

"I will," Atalanta would promise, feeling both irritated and guilty.

"I might could go 5, if we run slow."

"Okay."

"Or 4. I may need to build up. Are you sure you need to be running this much?"

"I'm fine," Atalanta would say.

And then here would come Hip with his two cents. "Would you like a running coach? I know one. I'll call him if you want."

That would be Hip, a non-nonsense kind of guy who specialized in handing out advice as if every problem could be solved. Easy. Like apple pie.

"No," Atalanta would say. It was her life. If she wanted to run her life into the ground, who were they to stop her? "But thank you, anyway," she would add, aware that that the bones of friendship might be strained but not yet broken.

She does, in fact, sincerely appreciate Val and Hip and everything they do for her, but she suspects they would not understand. No one would. It's like a secret she has discovered, a distance she can run beyond which she experiences a particular kind of pain, more than sore feet or tired legs, more than tight hamstrings or stiff hips and back, a peculiar all-over ache that makes her feel sometimes nauseous, and sometimes not, but always exhilarated. She suspects they would not approve. She's pretty sure they would not believe her if she told them this pain was a comfort and a companion. Especially as the pandemic stretched into months, and she stopped having anything interesting to say, since one day was like the day before and would be like the day after, and small talk began making her voice feel disconnected from her body, as she sensed herself growing vaguer, nearly paralyzed from a loneliness that she was not sure even a dog could cure. She found herself curious as to whether this is what it might feel like to disappear incrementally, the way running could feel like being erased, the pain, proof of erasure *and* proof of existence, the boundary lines blurring between exhilaration and negation.

Val and Hip, of course, won't let her disappear. They won't leave her alone. They want to thrust their hands into the void of wherever she is and pull her out, which, of course, they cannot do when she's running. When she's running, she's beyond the bounds of touch.

The phone rings. It is Val again.

Atalanta is sitting at the kitchen table after her 12 miles and a shower that was maybe too-long and too-hot and also, maybe perfect. She's limping a little. She has put on clean leggings and a clean tee shirt and a fleece. She's a little shaky. Hair still wet from the shower, muscles stiffening, stomach gnawing. She has fried two eggs and placed them on a plate with slices of avocado and a pealed navel orange and toast.

"What time," she hears herself saying into the phone, where she hears, in the background, the shrieking grind of the table saw.

"Six o'clock. The pie is in the oven. It's apple and it has your name on it."

When the woman from the health department asks where she might have contracted the virus, Atalanta tells her it could have been the grocery store, or the gas station, or that time she said yes to the dinner party, all because of an apple pie.

Ariadne

Theseus of Athens goes to Crete to kill the Minotaur, a monster who lives in the center of a labyrinth. (Thereby saving a bunch of virgins, but that's another story.) Minos, the king of Crete, has a daughter, Ariadne, who falls in love with Theseus and secretly gives him a sword and a ball of thread. He approaches the labyrinth, ties the thread to the front gate, goes inside the maze, stabs the Minotaur to death, and then finds his way out by the thread. Soon he heads back to Athens, taking Ariadne with him, but among the boatload of reckless moves he makes along his journey, Theseus abandons her on an island.

Here's what I did, I gave him $500. Not a loan, just a check, no strings, a lifeline you might say, and I *will* say because as far as I'm concerned, I saved that fucker's life. Five hundred dollars so he could get a new key fob to replace the key fob he lost by jumping into the lake in May when everybody knows it's too cold to swim, and he should have known better, only it's hard to stop a man from showing off when there's a pretty girl involved. He jumped off the boat with his pants on, so his wallet got soaked through and his keys, which he always wore half sticking out of his right hip pocket like some jingle-jangly ornament, slipped free and sunk to the bottom of the lake. Of course he had only one copy. If there ever was a second one, god only knows where it got to.

He didn't figure it out until we got to shore. After the shock of hitting the water -- *that* was a dumb thing to do -- he wouldn't get back in the boat until he swam around long enough to prove he wasn't that much of an idiot. By the time he scrambled back into the boat he was shivering, and we covered his head and his body with his shirt and sweat shirt and my jacket and Frankie's jacket along with two towels, but still he was shivering, so Beth gave him her jacket too. Frankie drove fast, which whipped up more wind, but we figured, the faster the better. There were blankets in the truck.

It was a scene like in some stupid movie, Theseus fumbling in his pockets for the keys after Beth and I stumble-walked him to the truck, me saying, *just hand them to me, already*, but when he leaned back and kicked the side of the front tire, and I knew something was wrong. *Goddamn mother-fucker*, he said, kicking the tire again, and I figured it out.

Also in the truck was the check. I mean, it was bad enough to lose the keys in the lake, and awful to have to leave the truck at the dock, but leaving that check was the worst. Frankie and Beth drove us home, but when they pulled up at my place, Theseus was so mad he didn't get out of the car. Just sat there slumped down in the backseat with his arms over his head, kind of half moaning every now and then. I got out and waited, but when he still didn't move, I shut the car door and waved. Frankie shrugged and drove off. Theseus's roommates could let him in, I guess. He didn't need his keys to go home, just to unlock that truck, where the blankets were and the check for $5,146, which he raised through his Go-Fund-Me campaign to buy food for needy people during the pandemic.

That's why I gave him the money. I was up half the night thinking it over. What I was thinking was, he could, and probably would, use some of the Go-Fund-Me money to pay for a new key fob, but that just wasn't going to be okay. All those people who donated that money? They didn't do it for a key fob.

The next morning I called him and was glad he didn't argue. I picked him up; we drove to the bank, and then to the car dealer. They said it would take about an hour to cut a new one. We could have waited, but I started getting those looks, like that thing that happens when people don't know what I am: Mexican? Indian? Some sort of Asian? To which I would like to reply, Tennessee. By way of Georgia and then Alabama and, for a short stint, Illinois, but mostly Tennessee. Except I'm rarely asked, only stared at, and these days with the pandemic it's gotten worse, like they're suspecting Chinese, and that's a problem with some of these folks. So we left the dealer and drove back to the lake to make sure the truck was still there. It was. And so was the check, in an envelope, sticking out of the cup holder between the front seats.

Long story short, Theseus got his new key and recovered his truck, and the check, and then what he needed to do was figure out how to buy and distribute all this food. I had assumed he'd worked that out. He'd gotten the people at his church to say he could use the parking lot, the church, I should add, where they were already running a food distribution program, which Theseus could have just helped out with, but as Frankie was always saying, there's the normal way and then there's the Theseus way. Even at the time it was hard to tell whether Frankie meant it as a compliment or a put-down, but I'm going to have to come out and admit that this sense of himself, that he could will things into being, was one of the things that attracted me to him. I hate to say it now, obviously.

The food he bought at Costco. I helped him pick it out, but that was the easy part. Harder was figuring how to get the word out. Even harder was getting all the permits from the city that he didn't know about. First he had to be convinced he needed the permits, and then he had to quit being all mad about it.

You're going to make me jump through these hoops just to hand out food to hungry people?

He must have said that 20 times to the woman on the other end of the phone.

Who told him, *yes.* Twenty times.

I didn't go with him down to City Hall, but he told me about later. *It's a goddamn maze down there*, he said.

Finally the weekend came. Theseus surprised his friends who'd agreed to volunteer for this thing by buying matching tee shirts and masks in a pretty spring green color with white lettering that said *Y'all Come Eat Now.*

Okay, as long as I'm telling the truth, I bought the shirts.

"You can't use this money for anything but food unless its toilet paper or toothpaste or soap. Things like that." How many times had I told him already? A hundred? A thousand? I got up to clear the table. It was a Saturday night, and I'd fixed him Korean barbeque, my take on one of my grandmother's recipes, and Theseus loved it, although he had to say the same exact thing he always said.

"It's good, darlin', but it ain't barbeque."

I'd quit trying to point out how stupid this was. And, honestly, I think if I had tried to speak it would have come out as crying. My dad had warned me that he knew a con when he saw one, but I was not ready to believe him, and sure enough, Theseus knew what to say.

"You know I'm joshing you, right?" he said, looking at me now and grinning in that way that made me glad I had not listened to my father. I smiled and put down the dishes. He grabbed me up and told me he'd marry me through a hole in the wall for my cooking.

I had made a spreadsheet to keep track of who was working where and when. Theseus had decided to open his food bank from 8 to 5 on Saturday and noon to 6 on Sunday, which was fine, but we needed to make sure there were enough volunteers to cover every station, but not too many, or there'd be all out chaos. The volunteers were mostly our friends but also people from the church and from the Bible study group Frankie and Beth had gotten Theseus to join. I went with them once, but Jesus Christ, the bullshit these people were spewing! I kind of thought Theseus would quit after Frankie said he'd had enough but, you know, I was wrong.

Theseus put me and Frankie out near the street, directing traffic, which I was glad to do because he was stressing me out. I mean, the first thing that happened was hardly anybody showed up, and Theseus started yelling at me – at me! – like was I sure I distributed all the fliers? "Like *all* of them, Ari?"

"Yes. Look in my car if you don't believe me!"

He was just embarrassed in front of his friends, I knew it, but still. It stung. But after about an hour, or not even that long, it seemed like the whole damn town showed up, and we were nearly out of food by 3. That meant we had to decide whether to close down early or break out the food we'd been saving for Sunday. It shouldn't have been hard to decide. There were people lined up in cars waiting right there in front of us, but Theseus had to go and make a big deal about it, ranging around the parking lot like this was life or death, and why did *he* have to decide.

It was Beth who broke through the histrionics by sitting him down and talking to him while I went inside the church and brought out another load of food bags. We got the line up and running again and ended up passing out food until nearly 9. In other words, a success, pretty much. But I finished the day thinking that Theseus, with his knack for willing things into being, might ought to think about willing himself some damn common sense. He finished the day by going over to Beth's for the night.

You heard right. Freaking Beth!

Frankie just shrugged and said, "Figures."

Figures? No, Frankie, it does not figure. It is true, Beth is a beautiful girl, if you like that pouty, anorexic white girl look, but Theseus likes his women smart, which Beth is not. I'm sorry, she just isn't. Go talk to her for five minutes, and you'll see. How many times did Theseus tell me I bewitched him? Well, evidently he got unbewitched, or there's such a thing as too smart.

Theseus and Beth did not bother to show up the next day, so I had to be the one in charge of handing out the small amount of food and supplies left, and managing the volunteers, and answering all the questions, like where's Theseus? And making sure that every penny of that $5,146 was spent in the way all those donors meant it to be. I'll say this, of all the ways I thought this thing might end, being stranded like some castaway on an island of pure humiliation was the last thing on my mind.

Arachne

Arachne was a weaver who challenged Athena, Goddess of Wisdom, to a weaving contest. Bad idea. She's a spider now.

Where had all the spiders gone? Arachne wondered. The wolf spiders that emerged from the woods behind her house every fall, or it seemed like fall was when it mostly happened, from what she could remember. She would walk into a room, say the kitchen, and see a spider, like a small hand cupped on the floor in front of the refrigerator, and she'd freeze for an instant, willing it to stay put while she hurried into the den and pulled

The Complete Works of Shakespeare off the shelves and then crept back to climb onto the countertop, or a chair, where she could gauge the angle to throw the book so it would land exactly on top of the spider. It was the best way, the most efficient and safest. Some people might think they could walk over to a wolf spider and step on it, but Arachne knew they could jump. She had seen it with her own eyes one morning when, rashly, she chose to battle with a broom instead of a book, and the spider jumped, not *away* from her and her silly broom, but *toward* her. Step on a wolf spider and you risk having it jump on your leg, or wrap its legs around your foot, or who knows what. The horrors that Arachne associated with the skills of a wolf spider were unlimited. But not this year, evidently. So where were they?

It was the wildest thing; her body seemed to be conditioned to look for them as soon as the temperature began to drop. She might not have noticed but for the fact that she was all of a sudden at home, all day and all night, every day, just about. Instinctively, she felt her eyes scanning the floors when she walked from one room to another. She dared not reach into the laundry basket willy-nilly to pick up a pile of dirty clothes. Before putting on shoes she would turn them heel side down and shake hard because she'd heard wolf spiders like to hide inside shoes. That she'd been spared this particular horror so far did not mean it couldn't still happen. Now that she was noticing, she couldn't remember when was the last time she'd seen a wolf spider in the house, maybe not in several years. Their absence had not registered as something to wonder about until this being stuck at home all the time business. Was it a climate change thing? Was it chemicals on the lawns? Something in the air? She couldn't say she missed them, but where were they?

The virus was keeping her stuck at home. Also unemployment. Both conditions, she hoped, temporary, although the absence of an end date made her nervous, frightened, jumpy. There might as well have been wolf spiders in her house. She was losing sleep and gaining weight. How many people was this pandemic going to destroy? Was this a cosmic test, a time to weed out the chaff? She didn't know what was going to happen, and dread settled into her body like a bite of bread she could not swallow.

Arachne was a weaver of stories and poems that remained mostly unread although a few had appeared in scattered literary journals. She'd had more success placing long-form magazine articles online and in actual printed magazines and newspapers. What paid the rent was bartending at the Public House, but the Public House had closed down for who knows how long. How long is a pandemic?

Travel, of course, had also stopped, limiting her options for reporting on stories requiring more than a phone call. Before the pandemic, most of her work fit into the category of feature stories about quirky people or overlooked places or interesting societal trends, but occasionally an investigative piece would fall, as they say, in her lap. *Literally* was a word she avoided, but it was hard not to argue that the piece that had gotten her into so much trouble fell into her lap, *literally*.

It was such a stupid story, predictable to the point of risking cliché, and still she got caught like a fly in a web. Was it love, lust, greed, ambition? Phillip was a charismatic guy, no question. Magnetic, formidable, powerful, connected. Arachne had never worked in television. She barely watched it. She told him that the first time they met.

"So why don't I believe you?" he'd said.

See? Just that spark of a tease was tantalizing. Phillip was good. A pro. And the fact that he seemed to know exactly what he was doing somehow made him more, not less, attractive in those early, heady days. How could she have been such a fool?

It was the article she'd gotten published about the small town in east Tennessee losing its hospital that had drawn his attention. It happened that he was developing a documentary series about dying small towns, but mostly in the mid-west and north-east. He was woefully unfamiliar with the south, and this hospital angle was a new twist in a overlooked location in an expanding tragedy. Would Arachne be interested in an assistant producer position? Phillip opened doors. He was a door-opener, a broker of power and connection and money.

Yes.

Would Arachne want to meet up to discuss?

So much got tangled up together. She had gone to his hotel room, yes. She had been there before, in his hotel room, in his bed, yes, more than once, yes, but not the last night. That night she had gone to his hotel room, but it was to tell him she was quitting, him and the project, both, and that's when he forced her onto the bed. In me-too speak, that would translate into consent, consent, consent, consent, more consent, but then no consent, although what it felt like was rape.

She would have kept quiet. The initial feelings of being stunned, shaking, angry, confused, and relieved to get out of there, turned quickly into beating herself up for being so stupid, and soon she was accepting half the blame for whatever. Leading him on. Not fighting back. It was embarrassing. A humiliating secret that required stuffed-down, shame-soaked silence and remained un-spoken for two years, until she heard the same thing happened to Jenny. And to Trish and Libby. Women who worked for him and some who did not. Some who were willing to talk to her and some who were not. Nancy and Stephanie and Kate. So many. All except for Marsha, but then, who knows what's true when your job depends on it. The story, as they say ... well, it would have been wrong not to write it.

The Complete Works of Shakespeare sat on the shelf next to two volumes of the *Encyclopedia Britannica Dictionary*, A-M and N-Z. All three books are big enough and heavy enough to kill a wolf spider. She had scraped and wiped cleaned carcass remains from the covers of each one, although the Shakespeare got the most use because it was on the end of the shelf and easiest to grab. So many spiders.

She remembers opening her front door to find a wolf spider on the threshold as if poised to slip under the crack and into her house. She remembers the spider calmly crawling across the fringe bordering the rug in front of the television. The several staked out on the floor of the bathroom. The one in the shower. In the closet. On the basement steps. Then there was the time, driving to the cleaners, spying the spider, big as a fist, crawling toward her from the pile of laundry on the passenger seat. That spider was the cause of the ensuing collision. The nice man collided upon understood totally.

Shortly after moving in she had asked the landlord about getting rid of them, but the way he had looked at her, as if deciding whether to bother answering such a stupid question. "You live in the woods," he said, finally.

This was true. The house was at the end of a gravel driveway about 200 yards off the road with spurs that took off toward other houses hidden in the woods. At the time, she had a boyfriend who played the drums, so it was kind of ideal. Even after he took off it turned out to be a fine gathering place for friends who wanted to haul out a keg and build a campfire and throw up a few tents. By the time the pandemic hit, most of those friends were married and had a few kids and nobody much was having parties anymore, and so the house had turned into a kind of quiet and lonely place. More recently, the landlord had explained that pest control companies could spray for ants, roaches, silverfish, centipedes, and stink bugs, but not spiders. Spiders, he said, can simply tiptoe over the poison on their wily, spindly legs. The explanation, she appreciated. It also creeped her out.

Now she wanders through the house weirdly missing them. Not the spiders particularly, but their emergence as a sign of the changing season. Predictable. Reassuring. It was like cold weather; she did not welcome it, but it made her feel alive in the sense that, this is the way life is supposed to be. It's what you look for, what you learn to expect and to depend on. If now she were to see a spider on her floor, she'd be a little freaked out, but she would know how to dispense with it. She has no idea what to do with a world turned crazy, unpredictable and upside down.

She remembers the night in the hotel suite when Phillip instructed her to keep her shirt off while he made sandwiches, and she did. It might have/could have felt kind of sexy and even fun, but that's not what it felt like. It felt isolating, as if trapped behind some fogged up window where she could not see or hear clearly and so time seemed to slow down and she did not know how to proceed. It was humiliating. There was something in his voice that made the words sound like instructions, not a come on, but a sit and stay. They had eaten the sandwiches standing up, he with his clothes on, she naked except for underwear, but she can't remember what they talked about. Rather, what she remembers was not talking much at all. Weird, yes, but weirder to hear Jenny say, *There was this one night, when he made me...* Same story. And then Trish. Except in Trish's story, it was egg rolls heated in the microwave. How could she not have a follow up question or two?

When after all the interviews, she called him for a comment, he told her she was full of shit. She didn't mind. It made for good copy. Kind of funny, actually, when you saw it on the page.

It is not funny now when, suddenly, no one is returning her phone calls, her texts, her emails, and no one is responding to her queries except for a handful of carefully worded rejections. She is scared to count how many rejections.

It could be the pandemic. Everything is shut down. Everybody is frozen. The whole world has paused. Who can predict what people want to read anymore? But most likely it's the piece she wrote about Phillip. Four thousand, two hundred and seventeen words. Fact-checked. She suspects she broke a rule, some sort of rule she did not know was a rule. But Phillip broke the law. Didn't he? Wasn't it a law that he broke?

And what about Phillip? What has happened to him? He has been, not fired, but suspended. A temporarily fix, a vacation of sorts, further investigations pending, everybody cooling off, taking a chill break, chilling out, sorting out next steps.

For him. Not for her.

She had not known Marsha had pictures. Arachne and Phillip walking arm in arm, kissing in the park, and that one where she was sitting in his lap with his hand on her thigh, and she was laughing. She would not have predicted Marsha would have betrayed her. Perhaps, she thinks, she should include trusting Marsha in her list of mistakes, as long as she is counting.

Her first mistake: letting Phillip convince her she could be a big shot when, really, she never was going to be anything but an obscure and marginally successful writer.

Her second mistake: sleeping with him.

Her third mistake: leaving out of the story that she, too, had been a victim. A crime of omission. The reporter did not reveal that she was part of the story.

Yes, but. The effort it would have taken to explain consent, consent, consent, no consent! It was complicated. Nuanced in a time when no one has time for complication and nuance. And was the story not true? Her small part did not change the facts. The story was about Phillip, not her. Phillip.

Yes, but. How much credibility, really, can be afforded such a person who would omit such a fact.

Arachne sits at her desk, laptop open, but nothing to write, and all she can think about are the spiders that should be emerging in the fall during the second wave of a pandemic that had begun in the spring when she had published the story that she believed would be her ticket out of obscurity and into perpetual employment and prosperity. It is unbelievable. How can it be that she, not Phillip, is the one sitting alone in her kitchen, waiting for the phone to ring. She was right. She was also wrong. A web that is, and will forever be, tangled.

Echo

Echo was a nymph. She got on the bad side of Juno, Queen of the Gods, who took her voice and made it so Echo could only repeat what others said. Echo fell in love with Narcissus, but her speech made him think she was making fun of him. She faded away to the caves and the cliffs and the desolate places. Narcissus hardly noticed. He was so conceited that he fell in love with his own reflection in a pool of water, fell in, and drowned.

I quit talking on Tuesday. Narcissus came home, he said, what's for dinner, but he didn't notice when I didn't answer so I quit talking some more. All night, just about, I didn't say a word. The phone rang, once, twice, three times. He looked over at me. "You going to answer that?"

I shook my head, so he got up. It was a man wanting money for the Veterans. I would have said no but Narcissus promised twenty-five dollars.

This morning I'm drinking coffee two-handed in my green bathrobe when he comes into the kitchen. I look like Gumby in my green bathrobe. Narcissus was the one who thought that up and it was funny when he said it and I'd laughed, too. I am Gumby, leaning against the sink, holding the coffee cup with both hands, poking my face into the steam when he stops, banana in one hand, thermos in the other, and looks at me. "You okay?"

I nod, which is like talking, so he goes ahead and leaves. You can't keep this shit up forever, but you would be surprised.

I take another sip of coffee and try to think about what do I want to eat. Nothing. Not one thing sounds good. It's like I'm sick but not really, like a piece of gunk has got caught in my throat that might or might not make me feel like throwing up. But I'm going to have to eat something, I know it. Already this coffee's scraping against the walls of my stomach. I have got to think. Eggs are too greasy, but oatmeal can turn slimy, and cereal can get soggy. What I want is a cigarette.

In my purse is a pack of Marlboro Lights. I dig through until I find it and pull out a cigarette and snap off the filter. Loose tobacco rains down on my green bathrobe and I brush it off in the sink then bring the end to my nose and sniff. It smells like dead leaves and mud or old leather, it smells great. Hard to believe it'll kill you. I hold the cigarette over the sink and roll it back and forth between my hands, back and forth, loosening the packed tobacco from the grip of its thin paper tube. I turn on the faucet and wash it down the drain then throw the paper and the filter in the trash. Saltine crackers. That's about all I can stomach this morning, crackers and a cold can of Coke to chase the coffee during zoom time.

Juno makes us check in over zoom first thing because she thinks she's got to see us working to make sure none of us are sleeping late or otherwise shirking, and we have to be dressed like if we were actually in the office – no PJ's or sloppy tee shirts for the workers of Preston-Long Insurance! If Juno had her way, we'd still be going to the office, damn the pandemic, and more than likely unmasked. Juno's like Narcissus; she don't believe in masks. Juno's why I quit talking.

What happened was, Melanie shot me an email with pictures attached and a note. *For the Spartanburg case. I need it by noon.* Only she did not, in fact, need it until Friday, and she knew it, and I knew it, and she knew I knew it, but she just plain did not care. That's the problem. It's Melanie's mission to have fewer pendings than everybody else and she can't understand why it's not my mission too. I've told her a thousand times, first-come, first served, which is fair and does not mean me dropping everything every time she pitches a fit. I flipped her back an email pointing that out and then copied Juno so Melanie would know somebody else was clued in, somebody who could, if she had half a spine, back me up. Ha!

I'd about forgotten the whole thing when late in the day, here came a text from Juno. She had taken the email I'd sent to Melanie and thrown it up on a google doc and scheduled a zoom call so we could look it over together, just her and me. It took me a minute to figure this thing out. Instead of solving the Melanie problem, she was fixing to correct my sentence structure?

Yes, ma'am. That's exactly what happened.

Juno didn't call them corrections. She said edits. Just a few edits I might benefit from. She was sharing her computer screen so I could see how she would have written it. "That's better, don't you think?" she said.

I couldn't see her face, so I couldn't see if maybe she was smiling. I would have understood better if this was a joke. Honest to god I didn't know what to say, but it hardly mattered. Already my throat was shutting down, like if I were to open my mouth, my voice would crack and my words would get stuck.

I did try to work after that but it was hard and I was steaming. Up to here in bullshit and no shovel. What does she think, like I'm some kid, easily distracted, like I'm a kitty-cat she can play with? You got to hand it to Juno: that was some neat trick she pulled, I mean. That was one neat trick.

This morning there are seven on the zoom, Birdie, Chip, Ashley, Danika, Melanie, Juno, and me. Melanie's got a smirk on her face, and that's before Juno asks me about the Spartanburg case. Right in front of everybody. So, you know, I lost.

But I'm not talking to these people!

How about that! Is this a bit of giddiness I'm feeling? I believe it is. Like I've got a secret, or maybe a secret power, even. I give them a thumb's up in the chat, like I'm rubbing it in. Only they don't know I'm rubbing it in. Maybe that can be a secret too. I pull up the pictures. There are nine. It's different angles of a garbage truck with its nose through a wooden fence and its front wheels planted in what used to be somebody's flower garden. Squeezing in Melanie's case means I have to work through another sleeve of saltines and another Coke, which is my lunch again today. Nobody has to tell me that it can't be helping my appetite to be sitting next to an ashtray filled with the pile of tobacco from the cigarettes I've been shredding. I'm still working when Narcissus gets home.

Narcissus is pretty much not civil until he gets a shower and washes work off him, so I don't have to worry about not talking to him. I'm not quite finished when he comes back out of the bedroom. He looks at me. Looks at the ashtray.

"It'd be cheaper to smoke them," he says. Then he gets his first beer and goes back outside.

Lonnie's out there, like usual. Them two will drag plastic chairs from off the back deck to the driveway where they can sit under the flags, drinking beer and watching the neighbor's yard. Through the kitchen window I can see that the neighbors aren't anywhere in sight, so Narcissus and Lonnie are stuck with nothing but the empty yard to stare at, and the chickens. I would go out there and tell them to cut it out, Narcissus has got them kids too scared to go outside and play in their own yard, but I've already told him and he don't listen. Anyway, he's already yelling.

"I sure could eat me some chicken tonight."

He's not talking to Lonnie, even though I can hear Lonnie out there chuckling. He's yelling so the Sims will hear him.

"Some good old *fried* chicken," Narcissus yells it again.

"Finger-lickin," says Lonnie.

"And don't I know just where to find me some," Narcissus says.

That's when I notice he has carried the .22 from the bedroom closet into the den where it's laying out on the coffee table like a live wire. I go in there and pick it up and take it back to the bedroom where it won't be such a temptation. After a while, Lonnie goes and gets a bucket from KFC, which he and Narcissus eat in the driveway, whooping and hollering over how good it is as they watch the neighbor's chickens. By the time Narcissus comes in for good I've changed into my green bathrobe, which he knows means to leave me the hell alone. I eat a bowl of cereal in front of the TV. Narcissus talks to the TV so he don't notice I'm not saying a word.

These days I'm not much for eating or sleeping. To-night I'm still awake when I hear a noise like something got pushed over on the back deck. Racoons, probably. That's when I remember we forgot to bring in the bird-feeder. They're cocky sons-of-guns, raccoons. They'll keep stuffing their faces until I go out there and stomp on the deck and yell *git* and then maybe they'll slink away. Reluctantly. They ain't scared, is what I'm saying. I get up and turn on the deck lights. It's not a raccoon. It's a dog.

A big dog. German Shepherd big, lying down at the top of the steps, facing out toward the yard. I've never seen this dog before. He's black and tan, more black than tan with a white streak across his face. He turns his head when I crack open the door. Now he's looking at me, tail thumping on the deck. I take that as it's probably safe to go on out there. He's big, all right. He stands up, meets me halfway and sniffs my open hands and then my legs and then my feet, tail wagging to beat the band. But he doesn't appear desperate or nothing like that. Not starved for food or water or attention. I sit down on the top of the steps and the big dog sits down, too. By this time I've discovered she's a she so it's just us girls, sitting on the deck at night.

The spotlight on the side of the Trimble's house lights up their yard and ours and the Sims' where the chicken coop is, and all up and down the street. The whole neigh-borhood's lit up like they're expecting thieves. Light from a waning moon, half gone already, spills across the yard. I switch off the deck lights so I can see it better and sit back down to watch the moonlight and listen at the silence. I know I should go on back to bed. I guess I've been waiting for the big dog to leave first. I guess I don't really want her to.

After a while I get up and stand at the door watching the big dog who's watching our backyard. It's okay with me if she stays all night. It does not seem right to feed her, but before I go back to bed I take her a bowl of water. I can't see the harm in water. I'm not trying to steal nobody's dog or nothing.

This morning she's gone. I look everywhere but there's no trace. I take my coffee out to the deck right about the time Wayne Trimble is heading for his truck. He stops and whistles when he sees me. I'm in my green bath-robe looking like Gumby but you got to know Wayne: *bathrobe's* got the word *bath* in it and *bath* means somebody's bound to be naked and that's all Wayne needs to get his blood up. Wayne's crazy. Wayne's also an asshole. I shoot him the bird.

"Don't make promises you can't keep, darling," he calls.

I don't even know what that means. He gets in his truck and burns rubber backing out of the driveway.

Now one of the Sims girls, the oldest I think, is coming out of the house with a bucket. From here I can make out the pale pink mark on the last post of the Sims' carport, the pale pink mark that used to be red on the post that caused so much trouble. That's when it started, when Mr. Sims built his new carport, and because their driveway is about exactly on the line, Mr. Sims didn't have a heck of a lot of room to work with, so he couldn't help but stick two of the posts on our property. I'm talking inches here. Maybe not even that much.

But next thing, Narcissus and Lonnie are out there with the lot papers and a measuring tape. Lonnie measured and Narcissus wrote the figures on the back of the paint receipt. Then he and Lonnie spray-painted a fat red line from the street clear to Wayne's fence, a big red line defacing the bright white paint on those posts. Mr. Sims said he was going to sue. Narcissus said he was going to sue. Nobody sued. Mr. Sims painted over the red but it never really covered it, and everybody just stayed mad, but then Mr. Sims built himself that chicken house and put the chickens in it. There's no telling what Narcissus will do next.

It's kind of a pretty little chicken house. I watch as the Sims girl with her bucket opens the gate and slips in and you never seen such a parade of cluckers in your life. They have names. Fluffy, Poky, Pinky, Susu, Daisy, and Pearl. I told Narcissus the names so he'd see they're like pets, but he just said, "That's stupid." I don't mind them so much. Narcissus and me, we don't see eye to eye on them chickens. Or much else anymore.

Narcissus lost his good job at the aluminum plant last year before even there was any such thing as the pandemic, which came as a big surprise to him but not to me. He should feel lucky getting hired on as quick as he did at the lumber warehouse, but he does not. He hates the work and really hates wearing that mask, plus they keep his hours under 30, which don't add up to enough to support him much less him and me both. I'm the one with the benefits now. The one who pays on the mortgage and keeps the lights on and makes the car payments. I'm the one carrying us.

At this morning's zoom we find out Ashley's gone. Juno informs us that she made the difficult decision to resign in order to homeschool her children, since this virus has wrecked the schools. There follows a loose discussion – not about how *not* difficult that decision would have been, I mean, does anybody *enjoy* working for Preston-Long Insurance? But about how hard it is on kids, this pandemic. Hard on kids, hard on parents. Seems like everybody's got a story. I could speak up, of course. I could point out you don't need a pandemic for things to get hard on kids and parents, but I don't. It makes these people uncomfortable when I talk about my children. And by children, I mean Penny.

They don't know much about Hank, my oldest, born when I was 17 and dumber even than I am now. He lives up in Chicago with a man he calls his husband. I've never met the man. Hank was six already when Narcissus came around. Another man's boy. That turned out to be a blessing, because Narcissus has got to blame somebody for everything, and so it's easy to blame me for Hank not turning out right. Of course, Penny was his, but he won't talk about her, either.

Penny passed away four years ago from an overdose of some kind of opioid, could have been heroin, but what did it matter, in the end. Narcissus blames me for Penny, too. I don't mind. When your child dies, blame settles inside you like it's another vital organ, so whatever Narcissus wants to think is the least of my problems. Juno and them had to watch me go through the years of not knowing where she was half the time, and so I think they're just as glad I don't talk about it anymore, as if it might be contagious, what happened to her.

Want to know what's strange? I'll tell you what's strange. Juno letting all this loose talk about kids and schools go on for so long. Sitting here listening to this, I've had time to shred two cigarettes. Usually she cuts people off to get down to business. I'm starting to wonder if something's up when here comes a text from Chip.

Ashley didn't quit. They fired her.

Really? Why?

Beats me.

So Juno is lying to us. I look at the other faces to see who else knows we're sitting here listening to lies. Chip's not letting on. It's hard to tell who else might be pretending not to panic. Ashley's the third one gone since April, and all three seemed purely random, and that's what's got everybody on edge. It can't be not working hard enough, because Todd was a hard worker, and he was the first to go. And it can't be talking back to Juno, because Birdie talks back to her all the time. Why Ashley and not Birdie? Who knows? It's this randomness that's scary, and it's worse to be sitting at home, alone. Honest to god I don't want to be talking to these people, but there is something to be said for being in the same room with them. Solidarity is not exactly a word I'd want to use, but, you know. This way, it feels like we're being picked off, one by one.

Working in insurance is messed up enough. Nobody wants insurance. People buy it because they think they ought to, or somebody tells them to, but they don't want to use it, ever. Buying it is bad enough; using it is worse. And we don't want you to use it. It don't work so good if you use it. There's got to be more people buying it than using it or this whole deal falls to pieces. It pisses people off to have to buy something they don't want. To use it, they have to wreck their car or have a tree fall on their house and that pisses them off even more, so our customers are pretty much always pissed off. Pissed off people take it out on the adjusters, and the adjusters take it out on me. Melanie's the worst. Although sometimes, I swear, I feel sorry for her. She tries so hard to talk like Juno, to dress like Juno, to like the same things Juno likes. I have wondered if Juno sticks up for Melanie because it feels good to have a somebody worshiping you. It's a steep price if you ask me, but could be that Melanie's got this shit figured it out and she's the only one of us who's safe.

Narcissus has put up another flag. This one's got a snake on it. A snake. Narcissus is afraid of snakes, so you tell me. It's hanging down from a pole he's nailed to the side of the carport so now we've got six flags over our driveway: the Confederate flag, the regular American flag, two Trump flags, one navy, one white, an orange UT flag, and this snake flag. Any more and people are going to start thinking we're in the flag-selling business. He and Lonnie are sitting in the white plastic chairs, drinking beer, staring at the neighbor's yard, when here comes Wayne Trimble walking over.

"Grab a chair and a beer," Narcissus tells him, so he comes on inside. I take my Coke and step outside on the deck while he's helping himself to the refrigerator, but here he comes, following me. He winks. I ignore him. He whistles, and I would like to slap him, but then I see the big dog running out of Wayne Trimble's garage, straight toward us. The big dog is Wayne Trimble's dog. I can't believe it. Wayne has no business having a dog, any dog. His last one he ran over in his own driveway because his truck's so big, he can't see over the hood.

"That your dog?" Narcissus yells from the driveway.

"Yes, sir. I'm going to teach her to kill chickens. She's going to be a chicken killing dog," Wayne says, as Narcissus and Lonnie burst out laughing.

"Tell what else she's going to kill," Lonnie yells.

"Can't do that. Echo will get mad." Wayne Trimble is looking at me. He's grinning. "Echo here, she's sensitive. She's got sensitive ears."

I sit down, and the big dog sits down next to me. I scratch behind her ears. She leans her head into my thigh. Moonshine. I'm going to call her Moonshine after the way she rose up to me under last night's sky.

Wayne Trimble drags one of the white plastic chairs off the deck to the driveway, where I can just see the back of the three men, sitting under their flags. Next door, one of the Sims kids comes out her back door to shoo two of the chickens back into the coop from where they got out. It's the oldest girl I think, I forget her name. I want to say she's about eleven or twelve, a pretty thing, thin, with a long dark braid down her back. She doesn't look like anybody from around here, and what I think rankles Narcissus more than the carport or the chickens is, he don't know what they are. They could be some kind of black, but they don't look black. Narcissus says they look like mongrels. Lonnie sometimes tries to guess.

"Could be some kind of Indian," he'll say. "Some kind of Arab."

When they moved in, Mrs. Sims told me they'd come from New Jersey.

"Hell, that's bad enough," Narcissus said when I told him. I'm guessing if her mother knew the girl was outside by herself she would make her come inside, but the chickens are loose and somebody has got to chase them down and the Sims girl seems to be able to do that while ignoring the three men next door sitting in their white plastic chairs, making stupid comments.

"I hate chickens," Wayne says.

"You and me, both, brother. You and me both," Narcissus says.

"And me," says Lonnie.

"So what are we going to do about it?" Narcissus says.

"I don't know, Mr. Live Free or Die," Wayne says. (Okay, that one made me smile. The only good thing about Wayne is, he's got Narcissus's number.) He says, "I would think you of all people would appreciate the right of a man to do whatever the hell he wants in his own backyard."

But this line of reasoning does not give Narcissus even a millisecond of pause. "You are forgetting that it matters *why* he's doing it, I mean, if these chickens are some tree-hugging, whale-saving, climate-whining asshole's way of proving he's better than I am, then I am defending my right to stick it up his tight ass."

"You tell 'em, Narco," Lonnie says, and Wayne raises his beer can in salute. "Can't argue with that."

"Environ mental case," Narcissus says.

"Now, if you fellows want to talk asses," Wayne says, waiting a beat, long enough to turn and wink at me *again*.

"You are a sick man," Narcissus says.

"Not looking for a cure," Wayne says.

He's grinning, Lonnie's sniggering, Narcissus is smoldering, only he's trying hard not to show it. He does not like to be upstaged by some loudmouth like Wayne Trimble who thinks he can come into his yard with his Mr. I'm-in-Construction biceps and drink his beer and talk shit about chicken rights. To me, all these guys sound the same, really, and the more they talk, the more the meld into one, like looking at your own damn reflection, you'd be hard pressed to tell one from another.

"What I could get into along about now is a big old plate of fried chicken," Narcissus says, loud enough for the Sims girl plus the whole street to hear.

Lonnie's slow on the uptake tonight. "I don't know. I kind of feel more like Mexican," he says.

I never have figured out whether that boy's crazy or just stupid.

Lonnie was one of the ones who got laid off six months before Narcissus, but to the rumors of a second wave of cuts, Narcissus just laughed. They can't run that place without me, he'd say. I don't know how Narcissus got to be this way, but he believes he deserves more, thinks somehow he's owed it. That's why it was such a blow I think, him with his good job, good pay, decent hours, benefits. He thought he was set.

People with money have people telling them what to do with it, and these people, the people who tell rich people what to do with their money, always recommend insurance. They say you got to have a cushion for this and a cushion for that and they can fix you up with car insurance and home insurance and health insurance and life insurance and disability insurance and umbrella insurance and long-term care insurance and trip insurance, but here's the truth. Money is its own insurance. When a rich person needs new tires, it don't take nothing but time to buy four brand new of the best, but to people like Narcissus and me, one new tire means we don't have money for the light bill. One hospital bill means we can't pay the mortgage. I know. Like the bill we got after Penny was dropped off by strangers in front of the ER, brain dead, but not yet dead. You better believe I know. There's nothing anybody can say to me.

People like Narcissus and me, we don't get the best lawyers money can buy. We don't have margins or cushions or peace of mind. We don't get to fix what's broken. This drives Narcissus crazy. He works hard and it don't matter. He tries to live right and nobody cares. Every time he thinks he's got it figured out, he don't. Narcissus has suffered one thing after another. A lot of it's come from that temper of his, and I've told him, but most of it's just lousy luck. Seems like there should be rules on how much bad luck one person ought to have to take. Or how much grief.

Me and Moonshine stay out on the deck long after Lonnie drives away, and Wayne Trimble stumbles home, and Narcissus sticks his head out the door to tell me he and Lonnie are going fishing for the weekend. From the deck I hear him turn on the TV news and then, in a little while, turn it off and go to bed. The house is dark.

From Wayne Trimble's house I have heard him whistle and call to the dog, whom he calls Fanny. What a stupid name. I can't think of a worse name for this dog. He has to call five or six times before she pulls herself up and plods across the yard, like what choice does she have. That breaks my heart. It's a terrible thing to feel stuck, believe me, I know. Lights from the houses crisscross the neighborhood. The waning moon is less than half now.

Lonnie's here already this morning when I wake up. It's Saturday, and I have slept in. Lonnie won't wear a mask, so I put mine on and make a new pot of coffee. Lonnie is looking at Narcissus and grinning like a maniac. "Did you tell her?"

"No."

Narcissus is clearly anxious to leave. He looks at the floor and then out the window. "All I'll say is, there's one less chicken over at the Sims this morning," he says. "I don't know what happened. Do you know what happened, Lonnie?"

"Nope," Lonnie says, trying, but failing, to stop grinning.

"But we thought you might ought to have a heads up, you know, if somebody starts asking."

Now it's Narcissus who's decidedly not grinning, but I guess the look on my face makes that easier. "I'll be back Sunday night," he says.

He starts to follow Lonnie out the door but then stops and turns to look back at me. "You going to be okay?" he says.

It does not take long to pack. A week's worth of clothes, and then we'll see where I get to. Maybe Chicago.

Or maybe, I don't know. I have always wanted to see the Pacific Ocean. Maybe I'm not thinking straight, but I don't care. I find Moonshine tied by a chain to a metal post stuck in the yard next to the garage door, which has been cracked open at the bottom in case she wants to go inside. It's nothing to free her, just a matter of taking her collar off. She jumps in my car like she's always been my dog.

First stop, the bank, where I guess I'll leave Narcissus enough to get by on for a couple of weeks. I consider leaving him a note, something like, *don't worry about me*, but then, I don't think he will.

Callisto

Jupiter, King of the Gods, falls in love with the Arcadian maiden Callisto, who gives birth to a son. (Unless he raped her. Reading these myths, it's hard to be clear on this point.)

Juno, Queen of the Gods, is pissed off. Naturally. So she turns Callisto into a bear.

It's hard being a bear. Callisto slinks around the outskirts of Arcadia because it's impossible to socialize with people as a bear. When she sees her son, all grown up, she wants to hug him even though he's about to kill her, because, you know. She's a bear. So Jupiter turns both into constellations: the great bear and the little bear.

It used to be you'd hear her laugh clear down the hall. An eruption of what I'm going to have to call pure joy, and if you went down there to get in on a little of it, you'd nine times out of ten see her son was in there, too, laughing or at least smiling, depending on how many times he'd heard her say the same thing already that day. It might have been something funny she'd read or seen on the television, something funny somebody said, or a story she remembered from back when she was a girl growing up in Jackson, but toward the end it was mostly song lyrics. She must have had a hundred songs running through her head in those days, and she remembered the lyrics to all of them. Funny lyrics to songs she'd heard when she was a little girl so we're talking like 75, 80 years ago. Maybe the way it works is, when holes open up in your brain, it's stuff from childhood that floods in. These were some wild songs. I'm trying to remember some of them. *I Lost My Love at the Stage Coach Saloon* – that was one. It wasn't just the lyrics that were funny, either, it was how she'd make fun of them, like she got the absurdity of a love song.

Miss Callisto might not always have remembered what my name was or what she ate for breakfast but she remembered how to play bingo. Her face lit up when I'd tell her it was game time. She knew how to cheat at solitaire, and if I caught her, she'd giggle and ask for a cookie. She was quick-witted. Feisty. She'd cut up with me and some of the aids, but nobody got her laughing better than her son. It used to be, before the pandemic, he'd come three or four times a week and stay a couple of hours listening to the same conversation he'd heard the day before. He was a good son.

Holding a phone up to her ear wasn't the same. How could it be? It's not that she couldn't hold it herself, the problem was not her hands, the problem was she never understood how the phone worked, and half the time she'd hit the red button by accident and hang up on him, and anyway, it wasn't her phone. She didn't have a phone. None of us were all that crazy about handing over our phones to patients. Or I should say residents. We were supposed to call them residents, which was another kind of bullshit. But for her, I did it. It was just too horrible not to. He bought her an iPad so they could FaceTime any time she wanted, but we still had to help her use it, so it wasn't any easier. She could still laugh over FaceTime and make jokes and sing funny songs, but it got painful because she'd get confused, and then he'd get frustrated, and sometimes he got mad.

"Why can't I just come see her?"

"I'll wear a mask."

"Why can't I just put on a freaking mask and come see her?"

To each of his questions, there was no good answer. Them's the rules, was almost worse than not saying anything. And it was like this with all the patients, or most of them, and their families. So much yearning over the phone lines, too much yearning.

Then there was the mask thing, and that was a whole other problem. It was hard on her. Everyday she'd ask me, "Why do you have that thing on your face?" Several times a day, every day, every time I walked in her room.

"It's the virus," I would say, or sometimes, "It's COVID," or other times, "It's the pandemic," but whichever, she would stare at me, or not exactly at me but off into space, kind of, like her brain was working to compute, but not getting it. Same thing with the eating in the rooms and the no more bingo. Sometimes her son would stand outside her window so she could see him while they talked on the phone, but that could open another can of worms. *"Why won't he just come inside?"*

Virus.

COVID.

Pandemic.

Once I caught her crying. She was sitting on the end of her bed, alone in her room, dressed like she was ready to go somewhere: socks and shoes, slacks and a sweater over one of the blouses that still fit her. She was missing her son, yes, but she was crying because Mr. Jim had been flirting with her, and she had flirted back, and she thought that's why we wouldn't let her see her son. Like she was being punished or something. I tried to tell her, no, no, but it was hard for her to understand me with that mask, so I took it off real quick to tell her what she needed to know, which was, Mr. Jim died two years ago. She'd forgotten that. Her husband died 17 years ago and sometimes she forgot that, too.

By July she was slipping, I could tell. There was this look on her face when I handed her the phone, a minute or two of confusion in her eyes while she listened to the voice on the other end before she remembered it was Arcas talking. Her beloved son. They would talk about the weather. Or, rather, she would. She would look out the window and tell him if it was raining or if the sun was shining. On the other end of the line I could hear him rattling off news of the family, like which grandson or granddaughter was doing what. Not much, frankly, since nobody was doing much of anything new these days.

She would wait for him to finish. "It's sunny out to-day," she would say, looking out the window, repeating herself.

Or, *It's raining.*

It's cloudy.

It sure is a pretty day.

Now I can't remember when was the last time she told me the lyrics to a funny song. But then, we were busy. Theresa got sick and then Stacy, and once we had 8 out at one time, and they got me, who didn't know a Hoyer lift from a Heimlich maneuver, working as an aide which, you know, I was grateful for. Better than being let go. I mean, what actual use is there for an activities director in a pandemic? But even with all of us pitching in, it was all we could do to make sure everybody got fed and cleaned up, and still. We lost seven.

He was furious. He knew his mother was slipping, he could hear it on the phone, and it made him frantic, like trying to keep sand from slipping through your fingers, trying to hold on to what's still there. Once he just barely caught himself from crying, begging me over the phone to let him come see her. If he could just take her out for an hour, if they could just talk in the garden, outside, masked up. I was so tired. Yes. I almost said, yes.

He was angry but he was also scared. He did not want her to get sick, like I mean desperately. He made me promise she would not get sick. Having to go through this every single day with him made my job that much harder, but then, I guess, it was better than watching the ones nobody called after. They were forgotten before the pandemic and they stayed that way. Some of them were the first to die.

By September, she did not know who he was.

The teddy bear was the one sent to me in a box by the vet when Lucky died. I'd never touched it. I'd opened the box and read the note and couldn't take it, so I shoved it under some sweaters in the back of my closet where it's been for, what? Six years I guess it's been. I'd forgotten it was there. I found it the morning I went digging through my clothes to throw out all what I wasn't wearing and would not wear again. When I pulled out the bear, it wasn't my old dog I thought of.

When I gave it to her, she brought it slowly to her chest and hugged it close and snuggled it between her cheek and neck the way you do a baby. She wasn't saying much of anything by then. I could not remember when was the last time I'd heard her laugh.

I made him promise not to tell anybody. He brought his oldest daughter with him, the one who was named after her, Callisto. Everyone called her Callie. Over Facetime she had been a boisterous 10-year-old with the wit of her father or, maybe, her grandmother, but here in this room behind her mask, she was subdued. In her father's eyes I could see the struggle between anger and gratitude, and I could hear it in his voice as he thanked me, like through clenched teeth. He knew, I think he knew, it was not my fault, not anybody's fault, but it is not as satisfying to rail at the universe.

I get it. It is just plain hard to think of the time lost to forever when he could have been with his mother before she was lost. Or maybe don't think about it. Anymore I can't say whether or not it's better to leave it be.

The teddy bear was still in her arms. It seemed to bother him a little, of course, he did not know where it had come from, but he did not take it from her. Her eyes were closed. He leaned down and kissed her forehead.

I'd put more than a little bingo money on the fact that she did not know who he was, but I could not help myself. "She knows you," I whispered.

The look on his face; I knew, he knew I was lying. It took a minute. He looked over at his daughter and then back at me before nodding. "Thank you," he said.

And I thought, what harm is there in a little pretending in times like these.

Phaethon and Aesculapius

Apollo, God of the Sun, had two sons, Phaethon and Aesculapius. Phaethon was peeved, because nobody believed he was the son of the Sun God, so he asked his dad if he could drive the sun chariot for one day. Apollo agreed. On that day, the sun swung wildly around because the horses knew there was a weak hand driving them, and so Jupiter, King of the Gods, threw a lightning bolt and killed him.

Aesculapius became a physician. But he got so good at it that he started bringing people back from death, overstepping his bounds, you might say. And so Jupiter hurled another one of those bolts.

Aescula is not believing what she's hearing. She takes off her glasses and rubs her eyes and sits down at the kitchen table in a chair next to the window that looks out on the screen porch. She would like to put her fingers in her ears but she's on Facetime so Phaeth would see her do it, and Phaeth would not get the joke. Aescula thinks a lot of things are hilarious that other people don't. She has been accused of thinking she's funnier than she is.

Phaeth, as Aescula can plainly see, is not at home. She is standing on the balcony of a condominium in Florida overlooking the Gulf of Mexico. She is wearing a sleeveless blouse under her jacket, which is to say, yes, it's chilly but she's in *F-l-o-r-i-d-a* and she will dress like it, weather be damned. She is drinking a glass of white wine. Aescula pretends to understand when her sister insists she absolutely had to get away. Again. This being the third trip to Florida. But then Phaeth drops the news that she will not be getting that vaccine even when her age group comes open. As it will. Maybe even as soon as the end of the month.

Aescula does not have to ask why; her silence is loaded with the question, and Phaeth is quick with an answer. Because it can make you infertile, she says.

Sitting at the kitchen table, rubbing her eyes, Aescula runs through in her head the many reasons why this is insane. She has at her fingertips the data to prove the extent of the insanity and could the tick off the reasons one by one, but she knows her sister. Phaeth won't listen to any of that. Phaeth knows what she knows. So Aescula focuses in on the infertility bit.

"You're 58, Phaeth."

"I know it."

Evidently, this is not the point, as Phaeth proceeds to school her in a deluge of verbiage Aescula can barely sift through. The point appears to be that, if the vaccine can make a woman infertile, god knows what else it can do.

"It changes your DNA," says Phaeth, the event planner.

"No, it does not," says Aescula, the internal medicine hospitalist.

She could say, *do you know how vaccines work?* She could say, *do you know how a virus works?* She could say, *do you know how DNA works?* She could say, *do you know how a clinical trial works?* She could say, *do you understand the meaning of the word, pandemic?* But there's no point. She does not, in fact, have to say anything, because Phaeth is all too familiar with the air of superiority that Aescula achieves with that way she sets her lips when she decides to simply shut up.

"I can't talk to you about this," Phaeth says, draining her glass and then reaching for the neck of the wine bottle to pour another.

"You are tempting fate," Aescula says.

"You are a busy body," Phaeth says, before hanging up.

Looking at the screen porch reminds Aescula that she should have taken the cushions in for the winter. She thinks about it every time she looks out the window but it always feels like one more thing she does not have time or energy for. Everything these days seems to take more time and energy. But spring is coming, and with it the pollen, and she'd better get those cushions inside or she'll have a mess on her hands. With spring will come the chance to invite friends over for drinks and dinner again. Friends who have been vaccinated, of course. Would she consider inviting Phaeth and Mike to dinner?

Ben would. Her husband had never been as vigilant regarding the virus, and between them there had been a fair amount of teasing because of it. He called her the COVID Vigilante once in a rare moment when he was the one who thought he was funnier than he was. She had gone along with the joke, that didn't really feel like a joke, because it was better than arguing. When pressed, Ben agrees with her on the public health measures required to fight this pandemic, but he also listens to his partners who listen to FOX News, and so he's gotten good at hedging.

Phaeth already had the virus; of course she did. A mildish case, but still. It could have been serious. Phaeth was just lucky. It wasn't the mask thing, Phaeth was fine with masks, in fact, she and her girlfriends had started making them last spring and by now she had collected dozens in cute colors and patterns, like another fashion accessory, a mask for every outfit. And she wore them, too, over her nose *and* her mouth. But she could not abide the social distancing thing and simply did not see why she had to change her life over a virus. She saw who she wanted to see, when and wherever she wanted to see them. Listen. You don't keep Phaeth from her dinner parties.

It's these same girlfriends she's in Florida with now. Do they understand the concept of a bubble? Are they going to take the risk of eating *inside* a restaurant in Florida? Will any of *them* be refusing the vaccine? Aescula feels as if she has a good grip on understanding ripple effects. And statistics. And exponential growth.

She'll concede she might be a tad biased.

She is aware that she could be more patient, as Ben likes to mention, like every other day. Ben, the ophthalmologist, has patients who are not sick and not dying, but they are also not showing up for their appointments. He won't come out and admit it, but his primary concern since the beginning has been coaxing a reticent population to go see the eye doctor. Business is down. She gets it; he's impatient, almost to the point of saying, enough already. If this pandemic has revealed anything, it is differences in risk tolerance.

But the vaccine is different. She understands why Phaeth insists on hopping down to Florida every other minute, but never in a million years would she have guessed that she'd refuse the vaccine. What on earth for?

When can I get vaccinated, how, and where?

It's all anybody's been talking about for months, like the country's been holding its breath and now, finally!

There's a chance to breathe. Everybody she knows has a story to tell about waiting in line for hours, or getting up at 3 AM to get in a line, or driving to some far flung rural county health department, or refreshing the internet browser every five minutes, just to get that first shot and the precious card with a date written on it for the second shot. Everybody she knows except her own sister.

The next day, Aescula is dragging the porch cushions down to the basement when Mike calls. Phaeth's husband is not in Florida with the girlfriends, but is now packing a bag to fly down there because Phaeth fell and now she's in the hospital.

"Wait, what do you mean, she fell," Aescula says.

"I don't know exactly," Mike says. "Something about some sort of wall between the parking lot and the beach, but I'm not clear whether she tripped over it or fell off it. It didn't sound like a particularly high wall, just a weird fall. Enough to break her ankle."

"Break or sprain?"

"She said broke."

Mike promises to call as soon as he knows more, although it crosses Aescula's mind that Phaeth could call if she wanted.

Unless she was already in surgery or knocked out on pain meds, and now Aescula is feeling like a witch and hoping that she has not somehow jinxed her sister with unkind thoughts. Which is, of course, insane, and she knows it. Jinxing is not a thing.

The break was serious and did require surgery. When she talks to Mike the next day, Aescula wonders if she should go down there, but he says, no, he's there, and their oldest Sarah is coming tomorrow, and they'll need more help when Phaeth gets back home, anyway. Aescula feels like a left foot. She feels restless and a little guilty and mad at herself for feeling guilty. She thinks sometimes it's her fault they aren't closer and she vows to try harder. But then, sometimes it's Phaeth's fault.

When finally she gets her sister on the phone, she has just gotten home from an 8-hour shift that lasted 11 hours, during which she watched two men die from COVID and admitted three more, numbers that, though tragic, mark a notable improvement since before there were vaccines. It makes a hard day less hard and less hopeless to see those numbers going down, and everybody at the hospital is feeling it. Like nobody's chilling the champagne yet, but things are getting better. And there's a sense that things are going to keep getting better, vaccine by vaccine. She needs a shower but she is eager to hear the story about the fall and to hear about the surgery and the hospital and the doctors and nurses down there, but when Phaeth starts complaining about her weight, Aescula does not know what to say.

"How am I going to drink wine if I can't exercise?" Phaeth says.

"What does the doctor say," Aescula asks.

"It's going to be weeks before I can even walk."

"True."

"This is going to wreck my diet."

"Maybe not."

"You want to know how fast this fat ass can put on 10 pounds?"

"Are they controlling your pain okay?"

"What pain?"

"You broke your ankle, Phaeth. You had surgery yesterday."

"Physical pain or psychic pain?"

"I'm talking about your ankle."

"I'm talking about my pants size."

"When are they saying you can come home?"

Phaeth does not answer. Aescula can't tell, but it sounds as if maybe she's crying.

"How can I help?"

"I don't want your help, Aescula. You don't help. You just nag."

She is aware that this is true. She is aware that it's particularly galling to Phaeth to be nagged by her *younger* sister. Who is thin. Like their father. Who was known to radiate warmth to his patients, but not to his family, and had a knack for making helpful suggestions sound judgmental. Aescula was often compared to him, although she argued that she made more of an effort to suffer fools. To the rest of the family, this was an exercise in splitting hairs.

"What I need is to get this fucking boot off this fucking foot so I can do my steps," Phaeth says.

"Maybe," Aescula starts to say.

"Don't maybe me," Phaeth says.

"I was going to say that maybe, as long as you're in the hospital, you could ask if they'll give you that vaccine," Aescula says. She cannot help herself.

Phaeth hangs up on her.

Aescula stares down at the phone. "I guess I deserved that," she says to Ben, who had been listening because she'd put the phone on speaker.

"You think?" He is shaking his head.

"What?"

"I don't know why you can't cut her some slack."

"It wouldn't kill her to cut back on the wine, you know. And the cookies."

"And me," he says. He walks out of the room.

She watches him go. She does not know what he meant. She is trying to decide if she cares. From the next room, she hears the television turn on. Looking out the kitchen window at the bare porch furniture, she makes a note that he has yet to thank her for bringing in the cushions.

She walks to the edge of the den and stands in the doorway. On the television is a nature program. The program is about cats in Patagonia. Big cats. She does not know what kind of cats live in Patagonia. Ben changes the channel. Now on the television is a man in a suit yelling at the camera. She does not know who is this man, but she is not looking at the television, she is looking at Ben. She knows that he knows that she is waiting for him to speak.

He says, "You hurt her feelings. You're right about the vaccine, of course you're right, but it's not worth it."

"You're right."

"But you're not sorry."

"I'm tired, Ben. I'm the one who's been going to the hospital every day, who's been taking care of COVID patients every day, who's been putting on a damn space suit every day just to watch people die. I don't know why you people can't cut *me* some slack."

"But you love being able to say that. You are doing exactly what you want to be doing, Aescula. What do you want, a medal?"

Ben changes the channel. Now there is a basketball game on the television. It's a pro game. Ben is a fan of college basketball, but not so much the NBA.

"What are you watching?" she asks him.

"Nothing," he says.

That's what I thought, she thinks, but does not say it. She does not say anything. She waits for him to turn down the volume on the basketball game that is nothing and that he may or may not be watching.

"What I want, Ben, is for people to cut out the bullshit and get their damn vaccines or this thing's never going to end. I mean, my sister's crazy, we all know that. She's a case. But there are a lot of crazy people out there. What if this becomes a thing?"

"Don't worry. People are sick and tired of all this; they'll get their vaccines."

"Not Phaeth."

"Enough people will. You can't make people do what they ought to do. Of all people who should know that, it's you."

"Why isn't this driving you crazy?"

"You can't know what other people are going through."

"What are you saying?"

He does not answer.

"Are you saying there are two sides to this?"

"Just forget it."

"Are there two sides to a house on fire? This is public health, Ben. Bone up."

She leaves him to the basketball game that may or may not be nothing, stomps through the kitchen, jerks open the door to the screen porch, and goes outside. It's chilly. She should put on a sweater, she thinks. But she is tired of the cold and tired of sweaters and ready for it to be spring, and the cool air feels good on her face, and what is that she hears? Frogs. She hears the season's first croaking chorus of frogs from the small creek in the woods at the edge of the yard. Behind the clouds, a moon is rising. It is full or nearly full, and over to the right, a planet. Saturn, maybe. Or Jupiter. In her haste to get out there for a better look, she forgets how many steps there are from the porch to the back yard and, missing that last step, she falls.

Baucis

Jupiter and Mercury travel around disguised as peas-ants. Because they look like peasants, instead of gods, everyone they meet is mean to them, everyone except Baucis and Philemon, a poor couple who welcome the strangers. In the myth, Jupiter reveals himself, drowns the rest of the town, builds a temple for the couple to tend to, and then turns them into trees when they die.

I thought the pandemic might cool folks down a bit, give them time to breathe and, I don't know, to think. I was hoping. You can find a bright spot in every situation no matter how bleak, that's what I say. It's what I tell my students and I have to remind them over and over because the littlest thing can send them into despair, and you would think to hear them talk that nothing will ever be right again. You can't think like that if you're going be of any help in this world. It's like getting stuck in a rut but, instead of doing something about it, you decide you'll never get out. Well, guess what; there's always a way out.

Maybe if the falafel guy hadn't made such a big deal about helping people. I know it wasn't his fault, entirely, but did he have to say yes to *all* the reporters? Passing out food here and there; everywhere you looked, there he was. Pastor Pete wasn't the only one who got his back up, but you could tell he was particularly irked. I mean, maybe the church wasn't doing every little thing we possibly could for people in need, but it was hard to compete with the falafel guy. Another thing that did not help was for the sheriff to park himself in the back pew every Sunday like he was taking names.

The problem was, the sheriff used to sit in the front with the rest of the political crowd, glad-handling everybody who got close, but ever since they opened in-person services back up, he's been perching himself in the back. So you have to ask why. Some people, at least, are asking. I'd kind of like to know, myself. This is the same sheriff who made a point of saying he would not enforce any mask mandate, no matter who said so. It was the county health department who said so. He didn't care. And he got cheered for it, like *he* was the hero! That's the part that surprised me but, as I try to tell my students, people will always surprise you, and isn't that what makes life interesting? Inside the city limits, of course, it's different. You can't step foot inside a store inside the city without your mask on, but out in the county, you barely need pants.

The church is in the county, so, you know. There's a few of us still wearing masks, but most don't fool with it, and that includes the sheriff, sitting in the back, taking notes, making people nervous. Half the congregation does not believe there's anything to this pandemic business, even though we've lost four or five to it, (and that's just from what I know), which is why some of us are thinking about going back to the zoom. Everybody's got their ire up one way or another, so people were on edge to begin with, and then they had to hear about this Muslim guy passing out food every other day, and wouldn't you know this would be the time I'd be needing to ask Pastor Pete for a favor.

When I was planning out what to say, my first thought was, *suffer the little children to come unto me.* I tried it out on Philemon, and he agreed, that's always a good one, hard to argue with. But then he came up with one better. *I was hungry and you gave me food, I was thirsty and you gave me drink, I was a stranger and you welcomed me.* Of course.

I'll be honest, it sounded good when it was just me practicing with Philemon, but face to face with the preacher, that would be a different story, and I knew it.

It's not like a middle school math teacher to balk at any-thing, but it didn't feel right to throw a Bible verse at a preacher. Like a dirty trick. And it's not like I'd be telling him anything he doesn't already know. He knows. At least I think he knows what's the right thing to do, even when he doesn't always say it out loud.

The truth is, there's probably not any one particular string of words that would work better than another. If he could just see the faces of Angel and Micaela, there wouldn't be a need for words. If he could just see. They are terrified. Every single day. They want me to promise that their mom won't get taken away, but I can't do that. The best I can do is find somebody who can help. Or might could help, if only they would.

The sheriff -- some people call him the ice man. By which they mean the ICE man. Because he works with ICE. Before he got himself officially hooked up, he *wanted* to work with ICE because he *wanted* to be one of the ones who got to round up immigrants and ship them back to where they came from, and he made him-self famous for saying he was prepared to *stack them like cordwood* in the county jail until the feds took action. To me it sounded like something you'd be embarrassed to get caught saying, but he was proud of it, and there was a whole lot of back-slapping in the front pews when it came out in the paper.

You'll forgive me if I say they reminded me of a gang of middle school boys because – and Philemon will tell you it's true – a lot of people remind me of middle school boys. Don't get me wrong. A middle school boy can be a lovely thing. For the most part they are sweet and tender-hearted, still carrying around remnants of childhood innocence and puppy-dog exuberance. It's just when you get a bunch of them together, they might need a mitigating force like the steady hand of a teacher to keep them from getting out of hand. A teacher or a coach, a mama or daddy, a preacher. To see grown men back-slapping and sniggering and whooping and hollering over somebody wanting to treat human beings like cordwood, well, it's hard not to ask. Where was the mitigating force?

Pastor Pete and the sheriff are buddies. I know that. Everybody knows it. The Pastor is in big with that whole political crowd, and most people think it's good they've got him around. Something's got to keep the politicians on the straight and narrow, as they say, but these days I can't help but wonder who's listening to whom.

I met Micaela first when she got to my class in 6th grade. Her English was perfect, but she'd been here since she was four, so I don't know why anybody was surprised. She would race ahead through the chapters, so I would give her extra work. Some kids would see through the trick – *you mean the reward for hard work is … more work?* And they would slow down to stay with the rest of the class, but Micaela only wanted more. She was hungry, and I mean that in every way you want to take it. By the time the pandemic hit, she was in eighth grade, and it was Angel who was in my class. He was as smart as his sister, I could tell just because I've been doing this for a long time, but he struggled. He could hardly sit still long enough to concentrate on his fractions, and I was starting to worry about him, but it was when school shut down in March, that I got really worried. I very nearly lost track of him. Angel never once showed up for the online instruction. It could have been a problem with internet access, but I suspect it was something else. Some of this nuance of the problem and any number of complicated issues I did try to bring up to our principal when we were working out how to turn school inside out and upside down, but there was just so much to think about. My concerns, as they say, may have fallen on deaf ears.

How creepy would it have been to have a camera on in a house where you didn't want anybody to see you?

I got around to visiting them in early May. We stayed out on the back steps. I kept my mask on. Their mom worked as a home health aide, and she was not at home, and neither was their dad, but Michaela said she would help Angel with the workbooks I brought over.

"Do you have something to work on?" I asked her.

"My textbook," she said, and ran to get it, but it turns out she had already finished it.

I handed them each a treat bag full of snacks and promised to come back with more math worksheets to keep them going over the summer. It was when I was turning to leave when suddenly Angel leapt up. Throwing his arms around my waist, he buried his head in my side. Slightly panicked, or more unnerved, I looked at Michaela. She had tears in her eyes. She said, "Can you help us?"

At the time, there wasn't anything I could think of to do, but I could not shake the sound of that small pleading voice and the feel of Angel's arms around my waist. Their father was documented. It may be that he was a citizen already, I never have been clear on this point, but the main thing is, he had left town – flown the coup, skedaddled, high-tailed. So what did it matter? I know people have marital problems, but honestly, who would leave two children with a mother who could be snatched away at any moment?

I finally got to meet her one evening the next October when school was more or less back in session, only I wasn't seeing a trace of Angel. He was in 7th grade, of course, so maybe it wasn't any of my business. I just wanted to check on them, and so I went over there. And she was lovely. Really. Which made it all the more heartbreaking to hear she'd been let go. Fired, terminated, pink-slipped. The man she'd been taking care of caught COVID and the family blamed her, even though she had tested negative.

"I never caught the COVID," she told me. "And he is okay now."

"Did he have to go to the hospital?" I asked.

"No," she said. "Nothing like that. His son, I don't think he ever liked me." She went quiet then and waited until the kids were out of the room to add, "He scares me."

"Do you think?"

"I don't know."

When a sheriff's car began patrolling the neighborhood on a seemingly random but regular basis, she grew more and more afraid to leave the house.

This was more than I had bargained for, I have to be honest. I was just a math teacher. All I wanted was to make sure the kids stayed up with their basics so they would not fall behind, and not just these kids. All the kids. But what we had here was a woman with no job and no clear way of getting one, and no resources, and no legal status to stay in this country, and two wonderful kids who needed her, and what did we need? An immigration lawyer, or some sort of immigrant rights group, or a social services type agency, or what? I had no clue. My first thought was to bundle them into my car and take them to my house, where Philemon was surprised for sure. Pretty much speechless for a minute or two before he got the picture. As I knew he would.

"Well, okay, then. Come on in, make yourselves at home," he said.

My second thought was Pastor Pete.

What was I thinking? I was thinking about the falafel guy and why weren't we doing as much to be charitable. Just that morning I'd seen him again on the TV giving out free food vouchers to hospital workers, and in the back of my mind I was remembering something I'd read about a church over in Morristown after the big raid on the meatpacking plant. You hear of sanctuary churches.

Surely Pastor Pete would know the rules, but from what I understood, you can't grab somebody out of a church. We are a big church. I mean, super big. There are Sunday School classrooms in there that have never been used. Was I crazy? I don't know, but as I try to tell my students, you never can tell which path you'll take when you follow your heart.

Face to face, finally, when it was just him and me, I decided to start with a hypothetical. To test the water, you know. Because Pastor Pete, he knows right from wrong, but like I said, he and the sheriff are big buddies, so. It's touchy.

"Have you ever considered what you might do if you came across a family, a good Christian family, who had never done anything wrong, but who might be in trouble?"

We were sitting outside on the bench that was dedicated to Jim McDuffie's poor wife who'd planted all the chrysanthemums but then died of breast cancer. "What kind of trouble?" He said.

"Like one of them could be deported."

"You mean an illegal immigrant."

"I mean a family."

"Why do you ask?"

"Just wondering if you'd ever thought about it. For a sermon, for instance. Or if you'd ever considered the ins and outs of sanctuary churches. It's in the news quite a bit these days."

"Yes, it is. But in your example, this family would, actually, have done something wrong by coming into our country illegally. They would have broken the law. Now, in terms of a sermon, there may be something in there to think about."

He had not finished murmuring about sermons and the process by which they are written, but I spoke up anyway. "Do you think the law is the law is the law?"

Pastor Pete looked puzzled by my question, so I added, "I mean, do you think there are some laws that are wrong?"

"Why, yes," he said, but slowly, peering at me as if he was trying to remember what all he knew about me. "But I'm not quite sure what you are getting at."

"I mean, would the church ever have an obligation."

"To whom? To what? Is there something you are trying to tell me, Baucis?"

You are going to wonder how this ended. Because Micaela and Angel are still with me, and those guys did come and take their mother, and the last we heard she was still in a facility in Louisiana, and even though we finally found an immigration lawyer to help, it does not look good. But I did not tell that man anything that day on the bench near the chrysanthemums. Pastor Pete is a young guy who looks younger than his age. Fresh-faced, eager-eyes, not a lot of backbone that I can see. And I did see who he was in the split-second after I heard him say my name. I saw that, if given a chance, he very well could do worse than not help. As hard as this is on everybody, and it is hard, really, hard, at least I don't have to live with any kind of guilt that I turned her in. Sanctuary churches, my foot.

But we got sloppy, and maybe that one is on me. Philemon and I managed to keep the family intact, mom hidden and both kids in school, until the spring when it started looking as if things might be getting better. Vaccines had come for COVID, that hateful man was gone from the White House, my students were getting back on track, and azaleas were starting to bloom. We took a Saturday and all went outside to plant a couple of trees in the back yard where our neighbors, who had not realized we had house guests, started asking questions that, frankly, we did not have good enough answers for.

Anymore it's hard to know when it's safe to let your guard down, and I guess, maybe, that's a lesson. Maybe the riskiest time for whatever might come at you in life is right at the moment when you're starting to feel like everything's going to be okay.

On the other hand, really? How's anybody supposed to live that way? It's no way to live, I know that much. But sometimes when I look at those trees I can't help but think about how people do things, thinking it's the right thing, when they don't know. And I don't know what to tell my students anymore.

Icarus

Daedalus built that labyrinth for King Minos in Crete, (the one Theseus found his way out of with the help of Ariadne). But then Minos turned against him, imprisoning both him and his son Icarus. Daedalus fashioned wings out of wax so they could escape. They were flying over the sea, nearing the mainland, when Icarus flew too close to the sun.

Icarus stole the candy bar. Everybody saw it. This time he didn't try to hide it. He waited until Mr. Bodie was looking at him before reaching for the candy bar and slipping it into his pocket. Mr. Bodie knew Icarus helped himself to candy bars and gum and cigarette lighters and fountain pens and anything else he could fit in his pocket every time he walked in the store, but it was only when he thought nobody was looking. Icarus' friends knew it, too, and some, like Andy and Bob, admired his cleverness at getting away with it. It took talent to be as sneaky as Icarus. Sometimes when they made it out of the store, sniggering and smirking, Icarus would share his stolen bounty. But not every time. Nobody expected him to do it right out in the open. With Mr. Bodie watching. Nobody would have guessed he'd just stand there smiling as he waited to see if Mr. Bodie would say anything.

Mr. Bodie did not say anything. This was too much for some of Icarus' friends, Sally and Peg and Andy, to name a few, who shivered at the implications. It had been scary but also thrilling to watch Icarus sneak a candy bar into his pocket behind the backs of grown-ups, but when the grown-ups knew and said nothing, then something was bad wrong. Off-kilter.

They didn't even know about the time Mr. Bodie had quietly mentioned the shoplifting to Icarus' father. Mr. Bodie had not used the word shoplifting when he spoke to Daedalus. Icarus "sometimes forgets to pay for things," was how he put it, preserving the veneer of innocence.

"You're thinking of someone else," said Daedalus.

"Of course."

"Icarus would never do that."

Not a lot of wiggle room there for poor Mr. Bodie.

So Icarus lost some friends, but he was not interested in friends who were not loyal. Sometimes it was beneficial to test his friends, cull the herd, one might say, as in the time in tenth grade when he asked Heidi to write his English paper for him, and Heidi said no. Good to know. Heidi somehow did not make it onto the student council the next year. Sam agreed to do it. Also good to know. Sam let him cheat off the math final, too, which turned out to boost his grade enough to attract the favorable attention of his father, but only momentarily. Not enough to shorten the ever-widening distance between them.

These were the seeds that grew the boy to the man. It is said that people can change, and this may be true. The opposite is also true.

Icarus might have gotten away with everything, two bit con man, small change grifter, real estate flimflam, money launderer, attention whore, belligerent, cruel, narrow-minded, paranoid, insecure, tiresome, childish, churlish, cut-throat, low-grade criminal. Except for the shining, blinding light of the presidency.

Gilgamesh

Gilgamesh, divine on his mother's side, human on his father's side, is the king of Uruk. He is the smartest, the strongest, and the fastest, but he's also a bully, and it gets to be too much for his subjects. He out-runs them, out-smarts them, out-plays them, out-parties them, and they are exhausted, and he is lonely.

It's a problem, and the gods decide to do something about it. They could kill him. Instead, they give him a double. Enkidu. Every bit as smart and strong and fast as Gilgamesh, but Enkidu is a creature of the forest, not the city. He speaks to the animals and they speak back. Still, he's pretty lonely too.

So to the virgin Enkidu the gods send a prostitute. Having sex with her makes him want to go to the city, where he meets Gilgamesh. They become best friends and go on all kinds of adventures together. Like they kill a demon, and insult the goddess of love, and have themselves a jolly time together, but after so much of this mischief they end up pissing off the gods. Again. The punishment?

Enkidu contracts a mysterious illness and dies. Gilgamesh is undone.

First off, he can't believe it.

Then he can hardly stand it.

Then he sets off to see what he can do to fix this stupid death situation.

Loosely, he makes three attempts.

Rejecting civilization, he flees into the wilderness, to live by himself and forage.

When that doesn't help, he tries the eat-drink-and-be-merry-because-tomorrow-you-will-die option, but that does not work either.

Finally he decides to find the secret to immortality and goes looking for Utnapishtim and his wife, (basically, Mr. and Mrs. Noah. Evidently there was a significant flood in Mesopotamia that inspired a boatload -- pun intended -- of stories over the centuries that followed). Utnapishtim and his wife are the only two people Gilgamesh knows who are going to get to live forever. But when he finds them, he discovers that they did not earn their immortality. The gods just gave it to them.

Not willing to give up, Gilgamesh puts himself through a series of failed tests, finally accepting the gift of a magic plant, which he promptly loses.

He's in the desert now, all out of luck.

But then, he lifts up his face and sees the shining city of Uruk. Oh my goodness, he tells himself. That's it. Life is with people. Since humans are mortal, the responsible response is not escape, hedonism, or trying to make yourself an exception. The responsible response is to work with your fellow human beings for the betterment of your community in the time you have left before you die.

So that's what he does.

Gilly and Eva

Prologue

The women are walking. It's the oldest story in the world, she says.

You mean love?

No.

Sex, then.

No.

Money?

No.

Treachery? Wait, I mean betrayal. Envy, hubris, greed, is that it? Greed? Truth, beauty. Desire? Or what's that, not empathy exactly, but...

No.

Compassion. It's compassion, right?

Death. It's death.

Oh, that.

BOOK I

She had seen everything,

she thought. She believed

there was nothing new to see, nothing more to know.

Before Pandemic season and all the other seasons that tumbled and lurched and upheaved as if from an invisible mountain hurling visible boulders, that time when all was known, or was thought to be known, all predicted, forecasted, opined upon with righteous certainty, the time when it was possible to believe it was safe to say you've seen everything.

In that time of righteous certainty, she would stand in front of the four tall gleaming windows in her office and gaze out upon the radiant city.

See the office, achingly clean,

The warm wood floor, the rich red fringed oval rug with golden circles, the white walls splashed with sunlight from the tall windows, revealing

No dust.

No dust and not one streak upon the glass desk top.

One silver laptop, sleek and gleaming, embossed with one apple,

one photograph in a silver frame.

One pencil, two pens, one black, one red, stuck tips down in the blue vase she bought that summer in Paris.

Climb the stairs, following the click, click of her sharp heels.

Approach the division between hardwood and linoleum where the click upshifts to clink.

Walk down the hall, past the open doors of the cluttered offices where producers huddle, and assistant producers, and writers, and camera operators and sound and photography and make up and graphic design.

Note the difference between chatter coming from the complainers and the creators.

Observe the people who look up when she passes and those who do not.

Find the double doors that lead into the dark quiet of the studio where there is a small desk and a chair built for her by a craftsman she found in Southern Virginia.

Take out the blue notebook inside the one small drawer. On the first page of the notebook,

Read her name.

BOOK II

Surpassing all.

Slight yet strong. Solid, packed tight in slim short stature, quick like a snake strike. Smooth skin, blue eyes, hair the color of sunlight on birch wood, long and straight.

Her mother, recognizing the stubborn streak, called her bull-headed.

Her father, smiling, shook his head. Bulldog.

Daughter of the dashing silver-haired titan of unicorns, entrepreneur, financier, arbiter of winners and losers, who knew a winner when he saw her. Gillian, he named her, already hedging against lost youth.

Gilly, her mother said.

Gilly, winner of spelling bees, soccer games, debate competitions, class president, Homecoming queen. Summers in France. BA in marketing and communication where she learned to weaponize messaging. Three years with McKinsey,

naturally.

Winner of grants, so many grants, the queen of grants, doled out, dribbled out, bestowed (granted) to the worthy.

At the Station, they created a position for her.

At the Station, she doubled the budget, transformed the mission, made possible what once had been impossible.

Awe and fear follow her.

The Station is her possession.

Through it she struts, high-heeled and suited in one of ten short-skirted silk suits that vary only in color: black, periwinkle blue, navy blue, red, gold, sage green, dark gray, light gray, beige, and white. She never wears the same color two days in a row. She rarely wears white.

She does whatever she wants.

Too much white space, Gilly says when Amy from promotion presents draft ad copy.

Not enough white space, Gilly says when Amy, hoping to please, presents corrected copy.

Gilly has changed her mind.

Gilly changes her mind without admitting to changing her mind. The fault, therefore, must lie with Amy, visibly withering.

Up and down the halls of the station, behind closed doors, the jerk move is identified. Amy has been jerked around, like so many before her. Like welcome to the club, councils Lawrence, director of production.

Lawrence sees what Gilly is doing.

Lawrence says, don't take it personally.

Gilly does not concern herself with behind-doors talk. She perfects the art of keeping people on their toes.

In the breakroom, Kim and George speak in low voices about anxiety medication. They are not talking to Gilly who, reaching into the refrigerator for her kombucha, says,

Take a bath.

What?

That medicine is bull crap, she says. If you're anxious, take a hot bath. Unless you are fools.

They feel like fools.

In her wake, Gilly leaves people who've never before thought of themselves as fools.

This is Gilly, who knows everything, who has an answer for

Everything.

She walks into the art department where speakers hang from the corners of the room and where she gets ideas for clothes she'll wear on the weekends from people who don't mind telling her they've come to work stoned. To them she brings word of new music. Nobody knows how she does it. But Gilly knows who's dropping the new albums, who's going to be the next new band.

Gilly leaves expensive chocolate on the desks of the people who work in development.

Gilly leaves pink post-it notes for Laurence on his desk with cryptic suggestions written in tiny block letters. Laurence understands. They are more than suggestions.

Awe and fear, adoration and trepidation.

People hardly know what to make of her.

Gilly is beautiful. Gilly is confident. Gilly knows what she is doing. When Gilly walks in a room, people say, wait a minute. People say, who is that? People find themselves walking over to where she is even if they don't want to. When Gilly puts her hand on your arm and looks at you in the eye, you forget what you are thinking. Your mind is scrambled.

The money she brings in has made possible more programing.

For education. For the arts. For the documentary films people have been waiting to make.

Click, click, grants land in her hands. NEH, PBS, Ford Foundation, Annenberg Foundation, Women in Film Foundation, Sundance, Independent Television Service, MacArthur.

Click, click, click, she flings grants as fast as slogans.

Winners win, she says.

Nobody can argue with that.

Click, click, she struts down the hall, past the open doors of the cluttered offices where producers huddle, and assistant producers, and writers, and camera operators and sound and photography and make up and graphic design. She walks past an office where a person she's never seen before is sitting, a woman who does not look up.

Not there one day, there the next.

Like magic. Who is this?

BOOK III

Lawrence had gone looking for Eva.

He did not know it would be Eva he would find. He did not know her name would be Eva. He did not know she would be a she. He did not care.

Lawrence, director of production, works in an office that mirrors Gilly's with four tall windows on the opposite side of the station. He has a different view of the radiant city.

He is tired of the office and the windows.

He is tired of Gilly. He does not think Gilly knows everything.

Lawrence, director of production, depends on Gilly's money, but he does not work for Gilly.

Lawrence, director of production, is tired of the same old stories.

Lawrence went looking for someone with a vision bigger than the ideas swapped around the station breakroom, churning through the cluttered offices of writers and producers who had been listening to each other for too long.

He went searching through the halls of universities but did not find what he was looking for. He explored the newsrooms, the courtrooms, the guilds, the unions, the coffee shops, but he did not find what he was looking for. Then, in a bar across the street from a law school in a university town, Lawrence met a woman who told him about Eva.

He has to drive a long way. Out of the city. Over two mountains, across three rivers, through a deep pine forest to a small town, falling down, losing a long battle with entropy.

She is standing on a second-floor balcony of an old brick apartment building overlooking a creek catching beer cans and plastic bags in the tangled roots along the banks.

She says, what do you want?

She does not ask him inside.

They walk beside the overgrown creek, stepping over beer cans and plastic bags. She tells him her story. But not the whole story.

He says, I hear you.

She says, I've heard that before.

He says, let me help you.

She says, you ain't got nothing I need.

He says, I've got money.

When Gilly walks into Lawrence's office, she does not have to ask.

He has been expecting her.

In Gilly's presence, Lawrence feels some of the fear but none of the awe. He knows a con when he sees one. He knows she cannot stand not to know.

Gilly cocks her head toward the office with the open door and the woman who was not there yesterday, but now she is. The woman who did not look up.

Gilly says, how much are you going to give her?

Lawrence says, as much as she needs.

Is it a documentary?

Yes, he says.

Do you know what it's about?

Not exactly.

What *can* you tell me? Gilly asks.

She has a vision, Lawrence says. And I think she might be what you've been looking for.

How do you know what I've been looking for,

she thinks, but she does not say it. Gilly wonders what Lawrence thinks he knows that she does not know.

Gilly says, Who is she?

Eva sits behind a large desk in a small office with no windows. She has chosen the windowless office. She has no time for windows. She is in a hurry. She is hungry. She is wild to tell her story. To get the story out. Eva cannot get the story out fast enough.

Still, Eva knows the story must be told right. No shortcuts. No distractions. Eva will see her vision through or die.

Someone is heard to say, exotic.

The secrecy is too tantalizing to ignore. Who is this alien woman from what unspeakable place, and why doesn't she speak, and why won't she hang out in the breakroom like everybody else?

Is she shy?

Anti-social?

Angry?

Is she wise?

Like a witch?

There are rumors of a brother in prison.

Also, a law degree.

Questions are not unwelcome, only deflected with vague answers, not wily, but deft, not stubborn, but unyielding. Here is a person who has arrived with no past. Who has walked in from nowhere. Who is standing up with no introduction.

Eva.

Tall and muscular, skin the color of sunlight on mahogany, eyes that burn like coal, a smile that has you hesitating even as it folds you into her, a smile that says, *do not concern yourself with what you do not know.*

Eva talks to Lawrence.

They're calling me exotic, Eva says.

They call all of us exotic, Lawrence says.

I'm going to be too busy for this, Eva says.

Stay busy, Lawrence says.

Gilly will not go to the office of the woman who does not look up. She will wait for the woman to come to her.

For one day she waits. For two days.

On the third day she is restless. She is angry. She walks up the stairs, past the offices from which some people look up and some do not, to the end of the hall into the art department where she gets ideas for clothes she'll wear on weekends from people who don't mind telling her they've come to work stoned. As always, they appear happy to see her.

It's hard to tell.

It cannot be examined too closely the fact that they do not ever happen to drop by her office with the four gleaming windows looking out upon the radiant city.

Gilly is careful not to examine this. She is careful not to notice they do not sit with her at lunch. They do not invite her to parties. They do not always remember to ask about her day. But they are curious when she pops through the door.

What's she going to do next?

Today she has brought them no new music. Today she is happy enough to occupy, for a minute, a space where no one expects anything more of her than new music.

She is in luck. Today is Jennifer's birthday. There are balloons. There are cupcakes. There is a bottle of prosecco. Jennifer, with the gypsy blouses, tattooed arms, and short hair, turns 26 today.

Twenty-six! Gilly is delighted to hear it. I loved 26, she says. Gilly is charmed. Gilly is exuberant. Twenty-six was my favorite year, she says.

Gilly tells people she is 29. She is 33.

Jennifer and her friends are thrilled. Atwitter with a new idea: can there be, in fact, a favorite year? And might it be 26?

Gilly is soothed. Pleased to have an answer to a question no one was asking.

They pour prosecco into Dixie cups and toast to 26.

Gilly raises her cup at just the moment when eyes shift toward something behind her. Someone. The woman who does not look up has entered the art department.

It's Jennifer's birthday, someone says. She's 26, says another.

Gilly turns around. It was my favorite year, she says, raising her cup again.

So I heard, says Eva, who is also 33.

What is yours? Gilly says.

I don't know yet, Eva says. Maybe 42.

Eva declines prosecco.

Eva follows Andy to his computer. He sits down. She pulls up a chair. He shows her something on the computer screen.

Gilly cannot see what is on the screen.

Eva is holding a manila folder tied with string. She unties the string and opens the folder.

Gilly cannot see what's in the folder.

Gilly is still holding the Dixie cup when Eva stands up to leave. Gilly downs the prosecco and throws the cup into the trash can.

Would you like a tour? She says to Eva.

Gilly leads Eva down the hall past the cluttered offices where producers huddle, and assistant producers, and writers, and camera operators, and sound, and photography, and make up. She opens the double doors that lead into the dark quiet of the studio where there is a small desk and a chair built for her by a craftsman from Southern Virginia. Gilly flips on the lights. She heads toward the set.

The desk sits on the set, raised like a small circular stage. Arranged around the desk are four beige chairs. Behind the chairs are planters in staggered heights for potted plants.

Gilly motions for Eva to sit in one of the beige chairs while she goes looking for a pitcher of ice water and two glasses. She pours water into the glasses and brings them to the set. She sits down at her desk. She smiles. Expectantly.

She is nervous, unexpectantly.

Gilly assumes Eva recognizes the set. It is a famous set, relatively speaking. Among the set of viewers that make up Gilly's world.

It is the set for *RACE: We're Talking About It!*

A groundbreaking program, where groundbreaking conversations take place every week. This is how Gilly describes it to Eva.

Friday evenings at 7. Six central. Conversations, discussions, arguments, truth, and reconciliation. An hour of television, groundbreaking, getting a lot of buzz, buzzing around social media and other media, waking people up, waking people the fuck up – as Gilly likes to say. It is Gilly's brainchild. Gilly's baby. Gilly's pet project. She does not know if this Eva is aware of all that.

Eva has not heard of *RACE: We're Talking About It!*

Eva asks, Is Lawrence the producer?

Gilly says, No. I am the producer. Why would Lawrence be the producer?

Eva says, I was just asking.

Gilly understands the question. She is white, Lawrence is black. Gilly understands that Eva may or may not have a point.

Gilly takes a sip of water.

She says, what's been amazing to me is how willing people have been to talk. I mean, really talk. Honestly. No holds barred. And it's not always fun, you know? Not always pleasant. Have you seen the show? It can get rough. Uncomfortable at times. But it is the only way we'll ever get to true healing between the races, black and white, I'm convinced of it. The only way.

Eva listens. Eva says, whom are you calling white?

Gilly is beautiful. Gilly is smart. Gilly is not always as confident as she looks. But when Gilly walks in a room, people say, wait a minute. When Gilly puts her hand on your arm and looks you in the eye, you forget what you are thinking. Your mind is scrambled.

Eva's mind is not scrambled.

Eva is beautiful. Eva is determined and unequivocal. When Eva smiles, she folds you into her. When Eva walks in a room, people say, wait just a goddamn minute. People say, who the fuck is that?

Eva does not believe she has to answer to Gilly. She understands it might be nice.

Lawrence says, it won't kill you.

White girl trying is better than white girl hating, he says. It helps to remember that, every now and then.

So Eva goes to the office with the four tall windows overlooking the radiant city and the red carpet with gold circles, and she sits in the chair with the awning stripe cushion, and she brings Gilly into the loop because Gilly did get the money, after all.

It is a performance, not required but expected, a win-win one might say.

Gilly just wants to know. Gilly needs to know, because that's who Gilly is.

Eva understands.

Eva tells a story about a small town, falling down, losing its long battle with entropy. She describes the overgrown creek catching beer cans and plastic bags in the tangled roots along the banks, and the hidden dump underneath the pine forest that is not hidden anymore, and the men who flooded into town throwing hush money around like chickenfeed.

She tells about the people in the town who take the money, who shut their mouths, who don't want to talk about it.

She tells about the people in the town who will not stop talking about it. The protesters, the resisters, the boycotters, the agitators.

She tells about the people in the town falling sick in statistically unreasonable numbers, and the doctors in the hospitals far from the town who agree: the numbers are unreasonable.

She tells about the sheriff, who pinned a bogus murder charge on neck of her brother, the loudest voice of pro-test, and about the sheriff's deputy who patrols the road like a troll exacting fees for crossing. The fees are high. Eva is not ready to tell Gilly about the rape.

That's another story.

Eva is finished telling her story. Now she waits.

Eva waits for Gilly to have an answer to what she has heard, because Gilly has an answer for everything, and because Gilly thinks she is white.

This is not what happens.

Gilly wants to speak but she can't think of what to say. She wants to smile but thinks better of it when she looks at Eva's eyes.

Eva's eyes are not smiling.

The silence between Eva, who is waiting, and Gilly who is thinking, feels awkward.

And in the awkward silence, Eva is surprised to find herself thinking, *Gilly is beautiful.*

People have told her, they say it all the time, but Eva never saw it. She never meant to see it. She never meant to be stirred.

Gilly does not say, take me there. She asks,

Can you take me there?

Eva hears the difference.

Eva is surprised. She wants to say, no.

Instead, she says, okay.

BOOK IV

Gilly wears no silk suit of any color. Today it is gray leggings and a lavender tank. She does not insist on driving.

For Eva, black jeans, red tee shirt with black fist. She drives a Honda Civic.

They have packed bags. They don't know how long they'll be gone.

As they drive over two mountains, across three rivers, through a deep pine forest, they find themselves laughing. Unexpectedly. Snort laughing, which almost never happens.

Which they had not expected.

Eva is not used to people getting her humor. She is used to people half-laughing nervously or frowning or furrowing their foreheads and pressing their lips together, afraid of saying the wrong thing. She has been unaware of what it might feel like to be in the presence of somebody as irreverent, as smart, as hungry to get what she wants. She has been unaware of what it might feel like to feel like she belongs.

Always the exile. The one who left.

The only one to escape the small town, falling down. The only one who made it to the university, where nobody knew what she was talking about.

Eva studied classical language and literature, which made no sense to anybody. Eva went to law school, which made only marginally more sense. After law school, she did not have to go back. After law school, she was the only one who went back.

Ever and always she found herself standing in one place, longing for the other place.

Gilly has been unused to being in the presence of someone who does not look at her in awe. She has been unaware of how great it would feel not to be both feared and admired. Like all the time. Like everywhere she goes. Unaware of how tired she has become of thinking that everything she does matters. Every word. Every move. Every decision.

Riding in the passenger seat of Eva's Honda Civic, Gilly feels layers and layers of giving a fuck flying out the window.

She feels giddy, listening to this woman, with no agenda, no comeback, no fast quip, and not one single answer. She feels giddy not to have to be the perfect one, the chosen one, the one who exceeds expectations.

Gilly feels giddy, not to have seen everything.

Eva and Gilly drive into the small town, falling down, losing its long battle with entropy. They talk to the man who has multiple myeloma, and to the woman who lost her husband to multiple myeloma, and to the son who lost his father, same thing. They talk to woman who lost a son to leukemia, the woman who lost a daughter to bone cancer. They talk to the man who lost his sister to ovarian cancer.

There is a lot of cancer.

On and on they journey through the small town, falling down, with the overgrown creek and the chemicals from the dump buried deep in the pine forest. Buried deep but not deep enough. Buried once, but leaking now.

They drive to the county seat where inside the jail house a man-boy was charged with murder when what he was doing was trespassing in the wrong place at the wrong time. The sheriff, wearily familiar with Eva, does not agree to talk to her.

I have been to law school and I cannot stop this, Eva says.

Gilly does not know what to say. There is too much to say. She does not feel like speaking.

She feels like screaming.

When she speaks, she whispers. This is the story of a country that does not love its people, she says.

No shit, Eva says, and then she says, are you hungry?

By *lunch*, Gilly thinks of small cafes with beet and goat cheese salads.

Eva drives to a Chick-fil-A.

Gilly says. We can't eat here.

Why?

You know why.

Because of the gay thing?

Yes, in a word.

It's good chicken, Eva says.

Gilly refuses to go inside the Chick-fil-A, but she is hungry. She will eat the sandwich and drink the Coke.

They sit on the side steps of a church. It is the Breath of Life Church. The name is on a sign in front of the small white frame building. The afternoon is hot, steamy, drippy, smothering, and they are sweating.

Gilly removes the top half of the bun from her sandwich.

Gilly says, I hate to say this. You are not going to want me to say it. But one documentary film is not going to fix this.

I know it, says Eva.

It's not going to change anything.

I know it.

Gilly says, sometimes I feel like we are, in every minute, all of us, barraged by a thousand words, a thousand pictures, a thousand films with words and pictures, and none of them break through. And we, who do the barraging with the words and the pictures, don't seem to know what else to do but make it a thousand and one.

Eva nods. I want them to see anyway, she says. I want them to see the faces. I want them to hear the voices. I want them to know who they are choosing to turn their backs on.

I want them to get a whiff of what it means to live in a country that hates its people.

Gilly has finished eating her sandwich. She wipes her hands on her napkin and puts it in the sack with the discarded bun.

Eva eyes the discarded bun. She says, do you have any idea how obnoxious you are?

Gilly says, I can't help it.

Gilly stretches out her arm, tanned to the color of pecan shells. She presses her deeply tanned arm against Eva's deeply brown arm in silent comparison.

Eva says, it's not just color.

I know it, Gilly says.

Behind sunglasses, Gilly squints up at the sun. She says, you are not going to want me to say this.

Eva says, you're going to say it anyway.

Gilly says, I love you.

Eva nods. I know it.

Gilly says, how far are we from the beach? She pulls out her phone, but Eva knows without having to look.

Forty-five minutes with a beer stop.

Let's go.

Gilly is beautiful. Gilly is confident. When Gilly walks in a room, people say, wait a minute. People say, who is that?

Eva is beautiful. Eva is tall. Eva is emboldened. When Eva walks in a room, people say, wait just a goddamn minute. People say, who the fuck is that?

Side by side they walk down the beach, scrambling minds.

Gilly is aware of exactly what they look like, young and fit and confident, walking down the beach, slowly, holding hands, caring not a bit what anybody thinks.

And can there be anything more audacious than a string bikini? Gilly's is yellow, a thin string connecting front to back across each hip, tied in a bow. One pull on the end of one string. Tantalizing.

One string ties the top across the back, another around the neck. One string lies flat across the hard sternum between two small breasts covered by two small triangles.

One pull. It's like a dare.

Eva wears red. A color like lipstick, you cannot look away. A bikini stretched tight over Eva's taut skin, revealing nothing.

Revealing everything.

She wears a hat. Floppy red felt, tipped slightly sideways.

Gilly wears a yellow bandana.

They could be pirates.

The ocean is rough. The waves, strong and curling, the current pulling left. Perfect for body surfing. Gilly will maybe teach Eva how to body surf.

Eva says, I prefer not to body surf.

Gilly says, let's check out the waves.

They walk into the surf, holding hands. Eva keeps her hat on.

They are chest deep in the water, beyond where the waves are breaking. Gilly throws her feet up, lies back, floats on the surface of the water. Over the top of her toes, Gilly sees the wave.

It is beautiful and gray, rising up out of the gray green blue water like a fist, like water turned into muscle, rising quickly, a moving wall.

Gilly thought she'd seen everything.

The top of the wave is frothing. It is curling. Gilly stands up. She knows, this wave is going to break on top of them. She decides to go under.

Gilly decides to go under, but sees Eva turn her back on the wave. She sees that Eva is going to try to outrun the wave. It cannot be outrun. Gilly knows. She screams.

DUCK!

What even does duck mean, she thinks, as she goes under the wave, holding her nose, coiling her body into a tight ball, feeling the wave roll over her, a powerful force, churning, buffeting, then gone, suddenly.

Frantic feet find the seafloor. She stands up.

Gilly looks for Eva. To the right, to the left, toward the shore. There is no Eva.

There is, in front of her, a second wave.

This wave is taller than the first. This wave is moving almost quicker than thought, but not quite. There is time to think, what is a rogue wave?

She thinks, I haven't made myself clear. She thinks, what is called for is precise language.

Gilly cannot see Eva, but maybe Eva can hear through instinctive connection, as if they are sisters. They are sisters. She screams, not *duck*, but

DIVE!

Dive UNDER the wave!

Holding her nose, coiling her body, the second wave churns over.

More frantically now she stands up. She scans the water. To the right, to the left, behind her toward the shore. There is no Eva.

WHERE IS EVA?

There is time enough only to think, do rogue waves come in threes?

Holding, coiling, roiling, churning under a third wave until it is gone.

Gilly stands up, hysterical and flailing.

The rogue waves are gone. The water is choppy, but the ocean is tame to the horizon.

Gilly fights through the water toward shore. She plunges her hands under the water as if to find a body there.

She screams, EVA!

In the distance, in the surf, she sees a red hat.

Don't you fucking tell me you can't swim, she thinks.

It is the one thought she has held back, because.

Because it might sound racist,

It might be racist.

But Gilly is not a racist, she is not. It is the one thought she has forced herself not to think, but here it has popped into her head.

She will not say it.

She would die first.

She does not have to say it.

Eva is found.

Eva, flattened by the first wave, got to her feet in time to swim under the second wave and then the third, as the swift current carried her leftward down the shore, where she is found sitting in the sand at the edge of the surf. Hatless.

Gilly finds her sitting, staring at the ocean, while the surf's edge rises and falls over the red bathing suit.

Eva is calm.

Gilly is crying. She is breathless. She is flapping her hands like birds. Oh my god oh my god oh my god oh my god. Gilly throws her arms around Eva's shoulders.

Eva sighs. Eva pats Gilly's arm.

Eva says, of course I can fucking swim, you jerk.

BOOK V

Eva has a funny feeling about this.

Gilly says, if you're going to throw a preview party, it should be for the people *in* the film, *I mean*. It's only fair.

Eva gets it. Eva agrees. But is it safe to travel?

Rumors of a virus whisper from afar.

What are rumors but a puff of wind. It's not like it's a *pandemic*, Gilly says.

Gilly and Eva, Eva and Gilly, they have made a film, and it is a good film. A great film.

Eva as creator, Gilly as financier, they are two sides of an unstoppable force, and they have become inseparable. On long walks they tell each other stories. Through long nights they talk.

Gilly wants Eva to tell her about Greek philosophers.

Eva says, let me tell you about Zeno of Citium.

They share their hearts. They tell secrets.

Gilly tells what it's like to grow up under the expectations of a titan of unicorns and a mother more beautiful than you are. Do you know, says Gilly, I should be in New York right now. I should be in San Francisco. London. But here I am. It's the best I can do. It is not enough.

Eva tells what it's like to grow up, the daughter of a broken man and a mother whose expectations include, *don't you dare.* I'm not supposed to be here, either, Eva says.

Parents, says Gilly. They think they're gods.

Nothing is off limits. They infiltrate.

What's it's like to be black?

Eva says, you don't want to know.

Gilly wants to know.

So, okay then, Eva wants to know, too.

What's it like to be white?

They are fearless.

They smoke weed and make chocolate chip cookies and eat all of the cookies. They drink gin and tonics and dance. Gilly flails about, arms, legs, knees, elbows, feet, head, hair, hips, moving un-synced. Uninhibited.

Eva barely moves,. Slow, steady, like sex if you pretend to imagine what sex maybe could be. She reaches out and touches Gilly's shoulder.

Slow down.

Gilly dances with Eva's boyfriend,

and when Eva acquires a new boyfriend, (because Eva cannot be bothered to keep any man around for long),

Gilly dances with him, too.

Gilly's boyfriend, the face in the photo on the glass-top desk,

is ditched out of boredom.

Gilly and Eva, Eva and Gilly, there is no match, no stronger bond. Two boats lashed together will never sink,

as they say.

One night Eva tells Gilly about the rape.

It happened after news of the dump had spread, and the doctors in the hospitals far from the town had agreed: this was way too much cancer.

On an evening when she was driving home from the county seat where she had seen her brother, the loudest voice of protest, in the county jail, held on suspicion of a murder he did not commit. She had been told, don't you drive that road alone.

His name was Darren.

Eva was driving alone.

Deputy Darren flashed his blue lights and pulled her over. Failure to signal. Paid for by the black body, still denied the right to walk through this world as free. She was 21.

The rape changed her mind.

The rape made her understand when she returned to her university that she would not be escaping into a world of Latin and Greek and the philosophies of ancient literature.

The rape sent her to law school.

Gilly wants to know what happened to the sheriff's deputy named Darren.

Eva wants to know why Gilly bothers to ask such a stupid question.

Now they have made a film.

The vision was Eva's, the money was Gilly's, there cannot be one without the other. A force, unstoppable, inseparable.

Except.

Eva cannot help it. She holds inside her heart a secret hope that the film, her film, might change the world. A little bit. Maybe. A nudge toward a more just future.

Gilly cannot help it. She holds inside her heart a secret hope that for this film she will be remembered. Recognized as truthteller. Change agent. Savior.

See and marvel at what Gillian has done for such a noble cause.

Gilly dreams of waves.

One night Gilly dreams of a journey, and in the dream she is driving up a mountain. The mountain begins to expand around her, and then the mountain turns into a giant wave. She is driving up the giant wave when it topples over. She is crushed. She wakes with the faintest taste of salt in her mouth.

Gilly toys with telling Eva about her dream but then remembers. Nobody really wants to hear about your dreams.

The next night Gilly dreams again of the mountain rising and turning into a wave and toppling, but this time before it crushes her she is saved by a stranger. She sees only the stranger's arm as it reaches in and pulls her out of the wave. Because of the stranger, she is not as quick to call it a nightmare.

The third dream is of fire. When she wakes, sweating, she thinks, *it's those fires in the news, that's all.* The terrible pictures. The terrible destruction. It sticks with you. Nightmarish. But later she reconsiders. Might it portend the subject for her next documentary? Fire this time. She makes a mental note.

She tells Eva about her dream.

Eva is not interested in making films about fires.

The forth dream is just bizarre. Again the stranger appears to save her, but this time it is from a terrifying creature, like an eagle. With a lion's head. Gilly has been drinking whiskey. She thinks maybe she should stick with wine.

The fifth is the second dream she tells Eva about. A giant bull, Gilly says. I know, it's insane.

Out of the city they drive, over two mountains, across a river, through a deep pine forest to the small town, falling down, losing a long battle with entropy, until they reach the elementary school cafeteria.

Tables moved to the sides of the room, chairs arranged in rows, a pull-down screen in front of a green painted cinder-block wall, a laptop set atop two encyclopedias on a podium.

All but a dozen chairs are full. A decent turnout,

Although Gilly had been expecting more.

I've been trying to tell you, Eva says.

Someone turns off the overhead lights.

The film is met with nodding heads.

The film is met with soft Amens. A few silent tears. Polite coughing.

Gilly feels pretty good.

She stands behind a reception table. On the floor to one side, a cooler full of ice and Cokes and Sprites. On the other side, an iced cooler full of beer and six bottles of champagne. On the table, sheet pans of pork barbeque, corn on the cob, slaw, cookies, potato chips.

The table is surrounded by people, and the people are smiling.

The people are cracking open beer. They are cracking open Cokes. They are filling plates. They are happy about this film. Grateful. They are saying, it's about damn time. They are shaking their heads and saying hooo boy.

Gilly smiles at Eva.

Eva has not left her place beside the laptop. She has been saying thank you to the people who have come up to her to say thank you. She has been smiling. Now she is not smiling.

The look on Eva's face, Gilly can't read it. She does not know what it means.

A woman is standing in front of Eva. The woman is talking. Gilly cannot hear all the words, only a few words, enough words to understand the equivalency of *who do you think you are*? Periodically, the woman jerks her head toward Gilly, the only white person in the room.

Gilly thinks she might be part of the problem.

The crowd that presses around the table with the barbeque and the beer does not stick around long. They have things to do.

Soon its only Gilly and Eva and the woman talking, and a man sitting in a chair, politely coughing.

They could have stayed over. They had packed bags.

Eva does not want to stay over.

They move the tables and chairs back where they found them. They pack up the laptop and the coolers and the sheet pans. They leave the elementary school cafeteria and get in the car.

Driving home, Gilly wants to talk. Parents, she says. They're impossible.

Eva won't talk.

Silence fills the car. They drive through the deep pine forest, across the rivers, and up the first of two mountains.

A gentle rain falls onto the mountain.

A gentle rain falls onto the mountain.

BOOK VI

Things are different at the station.

At the station, the awards keep coming.

Awards, prizes, acclamation, celebration, recognition, money.

Success breeds success.

Winners win.

Money makes money. And opportunity.

Gilly and Eva, Eva and Gilly, they are winners.

Whatever they want to do!

Mr. Patterson throws a party.

Mr. Patterson, CEO of the Station, who went to school with Gilly's father, but that was a long time ago. Mr. Patterson is pleased to host a preview party in the station lobby.

Blue carpeted, chandeliered, silver-trayed with canapes and champagne, open bar, no coolers.

Important people come to the party. They want to be seen with Mr. Patterson. They want to be seen with Gilly. They would like to want to be seen with Eva.

Eva makes them nervous.

Camera crews, assistant producers, graphic designers, and make-up artists make their way down from the second floor, following rumors of an open bar.

Gilly wears a pale blue suit, white blouse with yellow polka-dots, a welcoming smile.

Eva wears purple slacks, a lavender blouse, an expression that's hard to read. Nobody knows what she's thinking.

She is thinking, do these people really want to see this film?

After the film comes hearty applause, accelerated by competition.

Who can clap the loudest? Who can clap the longest?

After the clapping, the people don't stick around long. They have things to do.

After the party, Gilly, Eva, and Lawrence move upstairs to Lawrence's office.

They are drinking champagne. They are brimful with toasting.

Gilly the powerful.

Eva the wise.

Lawrence the patient.

Lawrence has been waiting

Because he is not merely the boss of people with ideas. He has ideas of his own.

He has been waiting his turn.

Lawrence has a story to tell. It is the story of two brothers who lost their land through the treachery of a system designed to take their land. Now he is staring at a budget big enough to tell that story. He cannot believe his luck.

Gilly, no one smarter.

Eva, no one more creative

Lawrence, growing a little less patient.

Lawrence is waiting to see if he can figure out if Gilly has changed Eva, or if Eva has changed Gilly. They are too close to tell.

Gilly in the pale blue suit, jacket tossed to the floor, shirt-sleeves rolled up, shoes off, perches unsteadily on the arm of a green upholstered chair.

Eva has untucked the lavender blouse and slipped off her shoes. She sits crossed legged in a black straight-back chair near the window.

Lawrence has hung the jacket of his navy suit on the back of his chair where he leans back, feet on the desk, sock-footed.

The party and the awards and the champagne and the toasting and the budget and so much luck should be making everybody feel hopeful, but Lawrence feels un-easy. There is tension coming from somewhere he can-not see, a dread he cannot name.

On the desk is a sculpture he bought on a whim at a street fair when he was a young man. It is a head, abstract, made of black glass with clay-red design. It is large but not expensive. Not a masterpiece. Not even particularly original, but it means the world to Lawrence. It has moved with him, from city to city.

It reminds him of the day he bought it.

It reminds him of who he was on that day.

He has placed it on a desk in every job he has ever held for 23 years.

A physical reminder.

Reaching for the bottle of champagne, Gilly knocks the glass head off the desk.

The glass head hits the floor.

It shatters.

From Lawrence's mouth, a choked wail. As if a soul could cry out.

Gilly says, I'm sorry.

Lawrence cannot speak.

Gilly kneels to pick up the pieces of glass. There are a lot of pieces. They are sharp. Her finger is pricked and she is bleeding.

Lawrence shakes his head. Lawrence says, please don't.

I just want to help.

I'll do it.

Gilly picks up her jacket. Eva stands up. Gilly says, I'll buy you another one.

Gilly the careless.

Lawrence the outraged.

Eva, not feeling so great all of a sudden.

Eva falls sick.

In the morning, Gilly pours coffee into a white mug in the break room. She walks down the hall to the small office with no windows, but Eva is not there.

Gilly carries the white mug with black coffee around the station, looking for Eva. She looks in the art department, in the dark studio. She walks, clink, clink, on the linoleum floor down the hall peeking through doors. She peeks into Lawrence's office, where Lawrence is not speaking to her.

She is surprised not to find Eva anywhere. She is also slightly miffed.

Gilly takes out her phone and calls.

I think I'm sick, Eva says.

Eva is still in bed. She has made it to the bathroom and back, once. She feels hot but cannot muster the energy to find a thermometer.

You aren't sick, silly, just hung over. Gilly laughs. Gilly is relieved.

No, I'm sick, Eva says.

Stay home, says Gilly. Stay in bed. What can I bring you?

Eva says nothing.

I'll be there in 15 minutes. What do you need?

Eva says, I am terrified.

Don't be silly, Gilly says. You're sick, not dying. You'll get better.

Eva says, I dreamed of dying.

Again Gilly laughs. Yeah, and I once dreamed of an eagle with a lion's head.

Gilly says, you almost died once already, don't forget. In the water, under the waves, but lightning doesn't strike twice, don't you know.

You don't know, Eva says.

For twelve days Eva is sick.

Gilly leaves boxes of saltine crackers, bottles of ginger ale, chicken soup in Tupperware containers outside Eva's door.

Eva won't open her door. Word's come of others who are sick, Andy from the art department, Mr. Patterson's secretary, a handful of people from the party in the station lobby, but no one as sick as Eva.

On the ninth day, the ambulance comes. The ambulance takes Eva to the hospital. Eva can hardly breathe.

Everybody knows what this is, by now. This is a pandemic. This pandemic is viral. It has a name. They used to call it Corona and make jokes about the beer, but the jokes aren't landing anymore.

Word's come that Eva's father has died from it already and her mother is sick in another hospital in another town a long way away.

Still, Gilly is not worried.

They say they know who is at risk and who is not.

Eva is young and healthy. Young and healthy is not part of the at-risk group. Eva cannot die. She does not meet the criteria for death.

Gilly does not meet the criteria for seeing Eva.

Eva is behind the doors of the ICU with the doctors and the nurses and nobody else. Gilly tries to camp out in the hospital lobby, but she is not allowed there, either. She tries to grab morsels of information from the doctor as she walks to and from her car, but the doctor is tired. The doctor is too tired to summon extraneous words.

Gilly wants to tell the doctor that Eva does not meet the criteria for death.

The doctor is not convinced.

Gilly wants to tell the doctor that the chronic stress of defending against structural racism ages the cells in the black body. Studies show. It might be important for the doctor to know about the chronic stress and the structural racism and the black body, but there is a risk to having an answer to everything.

People stop listening to you.

BOOK VII

Eva dies in the company of doctors and nurses.

Eva the creative, Eva the courageous, Eva the wise beyond her years.

Eva with so much potential.

Eva with things she still had to tell the world.

There can be no funeral, no gathering of family and friends, of followers, no collective mourning for those who loved her. It is shockingly small, the number of people who loved her.

Her father is dead. Her mother is dying. Her brother is in prison for a crime he did not commit.

There are a few friends, from the university, from law school, from the Station. Fewer still from the small town, falling down, losing a long battle with entropy.

On a Zoom call, Gilly, wearing a black silk suit, gives a eulogy.

Gilly clicks the red **leave session** button in the right bottom corner of the screen. She stands up. She knows where she can find someone who will sell her flowers, even in these days when the florists are closed.

Gilly does not know everything, but she knows a lot of things.

Gilly buys a dozen yellow tulips. She drives to the Station. The Station is empty. It is locked. No one is supposed to go inside the Station.

Gilly unlocks a back door and walks through the halls. Her heels click and clack and clink on the floors of the halls in the empty Station.

On Eva's desk in the office with no windows, she leaves the tulips.

As if that will help.

As if Eva will know that she was loved and not be sick at heart.

Gilly turns to leave but her legs crumple and she falls to the floor.

Gilly is sobbing. Gilly lies on the floor in the black silk suit and sobs.

She had seen everything. But she had not seen this.

BOOK VIII

Gilly drives home.

She goes inside and locks the door behind her. She closes all the blinds. She does not turn on the lights. For two days she gets out of bed only when she has to.

Gilly's phone rings, she turns off the phone. She turns off her computer. She does not see the invitations to the Zoom meetings and the Zoom parties. She does not care enough to decline. After two days, Gilly moves from the bed to the couch.

She does not turn on her phone.

She does not turn on the computer.

She does not pick up her mail.

164 - CATHERINE LANDIS

She does not need to have anybody explain what social distancing means.

Gilly perseverates.

Eva was not supposed to die... Eva was young and healthy... Eva was not in the at-risk group... Eva had so much more living to do... Eva was too young to die... Something has to be wrong with the universe for Eva to die... If Eva could die, anybody could die... Gilly could die... Gilly does not want to die... Gilly is too young to die... Gilly has too much to do before she dies... But Eva was not supposed to die... Eva was young and healthy.

And so it goes. Like a virus circling the brain.

Inside her dark and solitary mind, Gilly gropes for a way out.

Deep is the darkness with no light at all.

Inside her dark and solitary house, Gilly quarantines.

Deep is the darkness with no light at all.

Who can plunge into solitary darkness and emerge on the other side?

In the darkness and solitude, Gilly hardly knows the difference between noon and midnight, between Wednesday and Saturday, between April and May.

When she emerges, the streets are empty, the Station is vacated, her world has shrunk to a single question.

How shall I live?

BOOK IX

The silk suits stay in the closet.

Gilly takes with her a pair of jeans, underwear, toothbrush, and flannel shirt. She wears khaki cargo shorts and the red shirt with the black fist that once belonged to Eva.

Gilly walks away in a pair of sneakers with no socks and a backpack stuffed with granola bars, one knife, one flashlight, a candle lighter, a coil of rope, a water bottle, a small aluminum pot, a sleeping bag and ground cover.

The cabin sits at the end of an abandoned logging road, gutted and rock strewn, that follows a creek to a narrow valley between two mountains. From the east, the sun rises over the mountain an hour after dawn To the west, it slips over the mountain an hour before dusk. These are short days even in summer.

Gilly arrives in late spring, before the spring peepers. She arrives with a blister on her left ankle. Gilly has been told the door will not be locked.

It is not locked. Missing its top hinge, it leans sideways across the threshold, clattering against the frame when the wind blows. Inside is dark and cool. Grime opaques the windows. Clumps of leaves and mud obscure the floor. Something stirs in a corner. For a moment Gilly lets herself think, pest or pet?

The floor comes first. A thin broom leans against the sink. She sweeps, thinking,

How could Eva die?

I don't want to die.

Death is a stupid.

Gilly wonders, if grief is violent enough, might something fucking give?

The broom breaks.

The first night she sleeps outside, shoes for a pillow, counting stars.

In the morning, she fashions another broom from a stick scraped of bark, lashed with broad green leaves. She clears the floor of leaves and mud, and the nest of whatever that was stirring in a corner.

Gilly has blisters on both thumbs.

For a rag to wash the windows, she wads up a pair of underwear. She scrubs. She hangs the underwear to dry on the knob of the crooked door. She washes down the table and the two chairs, the small metal cot, the sink. No running water comes from the sink. She traipses back and forth to the creek for water, pretending she has never heard of giardia.

Gilly's blisters grow. Her back hurts. Her neck and shoulders and arms and legs hurt. Her cheeks are hollow.

Gilly is growing thinner.

Gilly is growing stronger.

On the third night, she moves her sleeping bag inside, making a nest for herself on the cot. Through the windows, she counts stars, thinking.

How could Eva die?

I can't die.

How violent can grief get?

On the sixth day, the man shows up.

Gilly is trying to start a fire with a teepee of sticks and her candle lighter. A bird has flown into a window, falling dead to the ground. She intends to cook the bird. She intends to eat it. It is difficult to pluck the feathers.

Gilly is starving.

Gilly sees the man walking up the abandoned logging road, gutted and rock strewn. She sees him stop at the creek bend. She feels him watching her. She does not speak to him.

Gilly thinks, if she tries to speak, flames will come out.

He says, I have brought tools.

She says, I don't need your fucking help.

He says, I'm not offering help fucking. Just a hoe. A hammer. Nails. Food.

He is an old man. It is his cabin.

He is the man the real-estate lady found by asking a friend of a friend's friend, after Gilly paid the disgruntled real estate lady $5,000 *not* to find a luxury cabin with gas range, granite countertops, and a hot tub.

The man replaces the hinge so the door will close. He has brought apples.

Gilly eats an apple and then another.

The man shows her how to pluck the feathers and cook the bird. They share the bird with hunks of crusty bread torn from a loaf that he has brought to her.

I don't know how to live, Gilly says,

This is one way, the man says. Not the best way.

From the east, the sun rises over the mountain an hour after dawn. To the west, it slips over the mountain an hour before dusk. These are short days, but getting longer.

The man comes once a week on the same day at the same time. He brings food. A large pot and a small skillet. He brings seeds and teaches her how to plant them. He brings news of the virus, spreading across the world below. He brings news of chaos and discord and churlish men with childish instincts.

They sit in the sun.

Gilly's cheeks are hollow, her skin tanned and sweat salted, her muscles corded, her long hair tangled and sun-streaked.

You are lucky, he says.

I have lost my friend, she says.

You have your youth. Your health. And more money than most, if you're honest.

I don't want to die, she says.

You have a fair bit of life to live until then, he says.

My heart is sick.

Mosquitoes emerge. Bees. Ticks. Chiggers embed in Gilly's legs. And poison ivy.

Dusk triggers the night chorus of spring peepers, crickets, cicadas. She watches for bears. The snake that lives in the woodpile stacked against the side of the cabin, she leaves him alone.

The man brings a bigger water bucket. Soap. Bread, eggs, hard cheese, more apples.

They sit in the shade.

Gilly's cheeks are hollow. Her lips are chapped. She has grown accustomed to feeling lean and hard.

Chosen austerity, the man says. Can't say it's the same as true austerity.

Gilly does not answer.

He says, I'm no expert.

Gilly says, if I die here in this valley, what will they say about me then?

He says, what were they going to say before?

Gilly does not answer.

The man says, before you came here, what were you thinking you were doing?

I was going to solve racism.

You?

Gilly does not answer.

The man clears his throat. The man sighs and then he says, You could maybe think about starting smaller.

The man sweeps his arm to indicate mountains, creek, cabin, and wilderness beyond. He says, the answers you seek, are you finding them here?

BOOK X

The yacht drops anchor inside a cove where the water is a deep blue-green. The sky is blue, pale and cloud-filled. In the distance, a white sand beach, dark green jungle, spotted with the reds and yellows of tropical flowers. The sounds of birdsong and surf are carried on the breeze. The breeze is warm.

Will this do? The young man says.

The young man finds Gilly in a bar where the beautiful people gather.

He is a beautiful man.

In this bar are people who might have known her father. And her mother. Some might also have known Gilly, or known of Gilly, but no one in this bar would recognize Gilly now.

Gilly wears dirty jeans and the red tee shirt with the black fist.

Gilly's hair is dirty, long, tangled, sun-streaked, rooted in a darker blonde. Her cheeks are hollow, her eyes blood-shot. Her face is puffy from tears.

Gilly is unrecognizable.

She is sitting in a booth in the corner of the bar. She is drinking straight Kentucky whiskey through a straw tucked into the side of her mask. She is the only person in the bar wearing a mask.

Beautiful people do not wear masks.

In the bar where the beautiful people gather, no one bothers to social distance. They press together around the tables in front of the windows that overlook the golf course.

When masked Gilly walks into the bar in red tee shirt and dirty jeans, people say, wait a minute. But nobody is tempted to walk over to her. No one gets close enough for a mind scramble.

Gilly is beautiful. Gilly is arrow-thin. But Gilly is no longer confident. She wears desperation on her face like foundation.

She does not want Eva to have died.

She does not want to die.

She does not know how to live.

She does not know what to do.

The question very nearly screams from her eyes.

The man stands in front of the booth where Gilly sits. The man is beautiful and kind.

Gilly pays no attention to the man.

The man puts on a mask and sits down.

Gilly says nothing.

The man says, You are too pretty to be this sad.

Gilly says, fuck off.

The man says, I can help.

Gilly sips her whiskey.

The man leaves her alone.

Gilly drinks her whiskey and also the whiskey the man sends to her table.

Beautiful people come and go. Gilly recognizes some of them. She could care less if they recognize her. She watches the man. He is beautiful but he does not mingle with the beautiful people. The man may or may not be aware that Gilly is watching him.

The man sits alone at the bar. He is drinking wine. Next to the wine glass on the bar in front of him, he has placed a book. The book is open and he is reading it.

Gilly cannot see the front of the book. She cannot tell what sort of book this is.

The sun sets over the golf course.

The man closes the book. He stands up to leave the bar. As he walks out the door, he feels her hand reach for his.

They are safe.

No one will die on this yacht.

No one has the virus on this yacht, anchored in the cove where the water is deep blue-green, where they have left the world of the virus far behind.

Where they have left the chaos and the discord and the churlish men with childish instincts.

Gilly and the young man have sailed away from sickness and death and chaos.

The man is objectively beautiful. He has thick dark hair and bronzed skin. He is fluidly muscular. He is calm. He is not worried. He wears linen shirts.

The man is not arrogant. He has no need to prove his intelligence. He has a superb sense of humor.

Gilly would prefer not to fall in love with this man, but it's difficult.

Gilly and the man sit on the high deck where the wood glistens and the brass gleams. The sun leans westward. The blue-green ocean turns blue-gray, stretching to what might as well be infinity. They sit on soft chairs.

From somewhere on a lower deck comes music in a minor key played on a piano.

Gilly places her bare feet on the brass rail next to the man's bare feet.

Spread across a nearby table are oysters freshly shucked, cheeses and pates, grapes, wedges of tomato drizzled with oil, slices of cucumber, olives, an assortment of breads, smoked trout, walnuts, pistachios, orange slices, figs, and an open bottle of 1996 Coche-Dury Corton-Charlemagne.

The man pours from the bottle. They drink. They dance. They are not in a hurry.

They sit on the railing above the blue-gray water.

Gilly says, my friend has died.

The man says, everybody dies.

Some people, too soon, Gilly says.

Still, everybody, the man says.

My heart is sick and I am afraid, Gilly says.

I understand, the man says.

I don't know what to do, Gilly says.

What then can be wrong with pleasure, the man says, opening a bottle of 1990 Armand Rousseau Chambertin.

The sun dips closer to the ocean. The clouds are rimmed in shades of red.

Gilly's hair is long and straight and clean. It is the color of daffodils. The cream-colored ones.

Gilly and the man dance again.

They perch on the soft chairs and talk of poetry, of art, of music, of language.

Gilly tells the man, I wanted to major in English but there was all this pressure from my dad, you know, to get a job. To do something useful.

The man tells Gilly, I majored in the Classics, Latin and Greek. I cannot tell you how they may or may not have been useful, but I am not sorry.

Gilly tells the man, Eva majored in the Classics.

The man says, life is too short to be sorry.

Gilly and the man talk about the majesty of evolution, statistics, and the clusterfuck that has been the response to this pandemic in their country. They debate the relative value between happiness and courage. They discuss, what is the meaning of life?

The man asks, does life have meaning?

Gilly says, I want to think so.

There is nothing either good or bad but thinking makes it so, says the man.

Hamlet, says Gilly.

You are correct, the man says.

Gilly says, I don't know what to do.

The man opens a bottle of 1978 Domaine de la Romanée-Conti La Tâche.

.

Laid out on table now, a platter of tuna steaks, rare, bigoli with basil pesto, grilled asparagus, fresh greens with pears and walnuts and blue cheese, bread.

Gilly and the man eat and drink. They laugh. They dance. They watch the sky darken and fill with stars.

Gilly says, I am tired of thinking.

The man says, don't think.

Gilly says, in this time of chaos, Eva would be helping.

The man says, Eva got sick and died.

Gilly says, I should be helping.

The man says, it can be enough to live for another day.

On the table are raspberry tarts with hazelnut crusts, custards of caramel and chocolate, almond cakes, fresh whipped cream. A bottle of 1959 Chateau d'Yquem. Shots of whiskey.

Below the high deck is a curtained room, lit with candles. Inside the room is a large bed piled with golden pillows and white sheets.

The beautiful man holds out his hand.

Gilly laughs. Oh sweetheart, don't you know by now, I am way too drunk.

Gilly sleeps.

Before dawn, the man wakes her, spreading her legs.

There are pitchers of water and cold glasses already on the table next to the bed.

The beautiful man brings her to climax with his tongue, and then again. Yes.

When the man enters, Gilly is ready to be filled with him.

Gilly thinks of Eva dancing.

Gilly shudders and cries.

The man covers her skin with kisses.

Gilly drinks cold glasses of water.

Gilly cries warm tears.

Gilly leans back on the golden pillows and falls asleep.

She wakes with the sun high in the sky.

Gilly feels the clean sheets. She feels the soft pillows.

She runs her fingers through her long straight hair.

On the high deck is a table with coffee, cream, juices, strawberries, peaches, mango, melon, pastries, honey, and soft-boiled eggs.

Gilly feels the sun on her skin, on her arms, still lean, still strong, and on her face, still with hollow eyes.

The beautiful man leans against the brass railing above the blue-green ocean that stretches to what might as well be infinity.

There are other coves like this. Other islands. The man has promised to never run out of places they can go.

The man turns to Gilly with the question on his face.

Gilly shakes her head. She is sorry.

It is not enough, she says.

BOOK XI

Una is done with talking to people.

She has talked to the reporters, she will do it no more.

She has talked to the doctors, she will do it no more.

She has talked to the politicians and the marketeers and the filmmakers and the hustlers.

No more.

Una is 96. She caught the virus. She almost died but then was revived. For seven days she laid in a coma, and then she woke up. She had survived when nobody thought she could survive. People said, it's like a miracle.

I have to talk to Una, Gilly said.

But Una is done talking to people.

Gilly thought she had seen everything. But not this.

It is hard for Gilly to believe everything she has heard about this Una.

Una survived the virus.

Una also survived breast cancer and colon cancer. She lost a husband to lung cancer, a son to Vietnam, a daughter to murder, a grandson to drugs. She survived. She lost a house to a hurricane. She hemorrhaged money to hospitals. She survived.

How?

Gilly must know.

But Una is done talking to people.

I'm not just people, Gilly says.

For three days and three nights Gilly travels by bus and then by boat to reach the island.

Near the beach behind a wooden stand she finds Ully, Una's son. He is selling tomatoes, corn, okra, beans, onions, peaches, and shrimp.

Gilly buys a sack of peaches. She sits down in the sand, takes a peach out of the sack, bites into the peach. Juice from the peach runs down her chin. Tears run down her cheeks.

Gilly is beautiful. Gilly is arrow-thin and tan and sinewy strong, but Gilly is not confident. Gilly's mind is scrambled.

Gilly says, my friend has died and I cannot bear this pain.

Ully considers this. He considers the steady beat of the ocean behind the dunes in the distance. He considers the sky, blue with fat white clouds. He considers the hollow eyes of the young woman sitting in the sand, eating a peach. He considers her tee shirt, red with a black fist. He considers how she does not throw the pit of the eaten peach into the sand but stuffs it into a pocket in her jeans.

He says, follow me.

Una is sitting on a bucket, pulling weeds from the dirt in a garden. She looks at Gilly.

She turns to look at Ully, her son. To Ully, she says, I'm done with talking.

You've said that, already, says Ully.

Maybe you didn't hear me.

I heard you plenty.

She looks like shit, says Una.

Nobody's perfect, says Ully.

Una looks at Gilly again. You look like shit, she says.

Gilly says, my friend has died. She was too young to die, and I cannot bear this pain.

Gilly says, and I am going to die, and I don't want to die, and I cannot bear this fear.

Gilly says, you are 96 years old. You are in the high-risk group. You have no more immunity against this virus than any other person on this earth, and yet you survived.

How?

Una takes this in. This question, she has heard it before. She does not have an answer.

Una is done telling people she does not have an answer.

Ully says, this girl could be anywhere else in the world she wants, but she is here.

Ully says, in her pocket is a peach pit she could have thrown in the sand.

Ully says, she has come alone.

Ully turns and walks toward the small house on the other side of the garden.

Una looks at Gilly. She says, I can tell you only what I know.

Una says, my son told me, if you get this, you won't survive. My daughter told me, if you get this, you won't survive. My doctor told me, if you get this, you won't survive.

Una grabs hold of a thin stalk of wild strawberry and begins to pull.

She says, when I got sick with fever and could not breathe, I thought, I won't survive. When they took me to the hospital, I thought, now I will die. When I fell into a coma, I did not think, I am dying.

I did not think.

I stayed in a coma for seven days. For seven days I did not know I was in a coma. When I opened my eyes, I asked for a Coke. On ice.

Why?

I was thirsty.

Una says, in the seven days I was in a coma, three patients in the ICU died. I should have died, too. I should have died but I didn't. The doctors do not know why. The nurses do not know why. I do not know why.

Gilly says, maybe it means you're never going to die.

Una looks at Gilly. I doubt it, she says.

Gilly says, you survived cancer, twice. You lost two of four children. You lost a husband. Your house. Your money. And now you have survived the plague. You have survived more than most people could survive. Surely there is a reason.

I don't know about surely, Una says.

Una's hands have found a clump of dirt. She picks it up and breaks it apart slowly so that the dirt falls back to the earth like rain. She picks up another clump.

Una says, nobody understands death. It comes for every one of us, sometimes fast, sometimes slow, but it always comes and it always will, for everyone, and still. We plant gardens, pluck weeds, raise children, build houses, sign contracts, go to school, go to work, go to movies, go to dinner. We make bread and music and art and love and war as if all of this will last forever. Look at the mayflies on the river. On the water, sun on their faces, they don't know they're flowing downstream.

Down the road come a gaggle of children. Gilly watches the children. Six children, ages from 12 maybe down to 3. The children are singing. Gilly thinks she has heard this song before but cannot place it.

Ully comes out of the small house.

Una points to three boxes sitting at the edge of the garden. The boxes are filled with lettuces, cucumbers, peppers, potatoes, eggplant, cabbage, green beans, and tomatoes. Ully picks up the boxes and carries the them to the children.

Una stands up. She blows kisses at the children.

She walks to a spigot next to a garden shed and turns it on. She washes her hands in the water.

Gilly watches Una. She asks, do you meditate?

Una says, who has time?

Gilly asks, do you believe in God?

Una says, ha!

Una turns off the spigot and dries her hands on her shirt.

Gilly says, surely you have faith in something.

Again with the surely!

Una walks to the small house and opens the screen door. She says, I have faith that the earth will circle the sun. Until it doesn't.

Una calls to her dog, a blackish, brownish, beagle-faced mutt. They go inside.

Gilly follows.

Una reaches her hands into a bowl filled with bread dough and turns it.

Ully comes into his mother's kitchen. He fills a basket with finished loaves and carries them to the screen door where a woman Gilly has not noticed is standing. He hands the woman the basket. The woman hands him a bucket of mussels. Ully brings the bucket into the kitchen and pours a bag of ice over the mussels.

Now Ully is cutting slices from the end of another loaf of bread. He places the slices on

on a plate with hunks of hard cheese and a handful of washed strawberries. He pops the top off three bottles of beer and sets them on the table with the plate.

Gilly sits down.

Ully sits down.

Una does not sit down.

Una takes a broom and turns it upside down and raises it into the air and brushes cobwebs out of the corners of the ceiling.

The bread tastes of the earth and of walnuts. The beer tastes like cold tears. Out the window, in the distance, Gilly watches a blue heron rise out of a marsh.

Gilly says, How do I bear this pain? How do I bear this fear?

Una puts away the broom. She says, You have a lot questions.

Gilly says, it's all I have.

Una says, Do you think there are answers to your questions?

Gilly says, I have to believe it's so.

Una says, If I could tell you not to believe what you already think, maybe then you'd be able to hear.

Una carries two onions and a wooden cutting board to the table. She sits.

She says, I have a question for you. Have you ever thought about how lucky you are?

Gilly says, funny, the old man in the mountains asked me the same thing. Yes. The answer is yes, of course. I am not a monster. I am not ungrateful. I just keep thinking there must be a reason for all of this. A purpose. Some freaking way to make sense of it all.

Una says, sounds to me like you're bound to white-knuckle that belief until you run out of breath.

Una's hands, the color of soil, peel the brown skins off the onions. She gathers the skins and takes them to a bucket sitting in the sink. She returns to the onions with a knife.

I'm sorry. Gilly says.

I know. Una says, everyone is sorry.

Una slices the onions into halves and then each half into slivers. She scrapes the sliced onions into a pot on the stove. She wipes her hands on her shirt. She wipes her eyes on her sleeve.

Gilly buries her head in her hands. Her hair, the color of pale yellow daffodils, falls over her hands.

Una says, Wait here.

From somewhere in the back of the small house, Una brings back a small box. It is painted blue and purple and red in uneven stripes. The lid is painted gold. A tiny hook locks the lid closed. Una places the box on the table in front of Gilly.

What is that, Gilly asks.

A box, Una says.

A magic box? Gilly asks.

Una shrugs.

I don't believe in magic, Gilly says. What does it do?

What are you seeking? Una asks.

Not a riddle, Gilly says. No fucking way are we doing riddles. She picks up the box and reaches for the tiny hook.

You can't open it, Una says.

What's inside? Gilly asks.

It won't work if you open it, Una says.

Gilly says, I don't believe in magic.

Una nods. She picks up the box to take it away.

Gilly says,

Wait.

Una returns the box to the table. They stare at it.

Gilly whispers, will it help me bear this pain? Will it help me bear this fear?

Una says, you came to me with questions. I am giving you this box.

Gilly takes the box into her hands. She holds it to her chest. She closes her eyes.

Don't open it, Una says.

BOOK XII

Gilly takes the boat and then the bus to return to the radiant city. In her lap she holds the box. She holds it close. She turns the box so the tiny lock faces away from her face.

Gilly does not want to look at it. She does not want to touch it. She believes the urge to open the box is a test. She does not want to fail the test.

The sun coming through the windows of the bus reveals the gold on the lid of the box to be a garish shade of gold. Pseudo-sparkly. Splotchy, as if painted by a child.

Gilly's fingers inch toward the tiny hook. Her fingers move the hook in and out of the latch. It would be awfully easy to open.

The bus is traveling down a state highway, passing through a landscape of empty fields, a monotony of hay and grass under a white-blue sky.

It is a world without people.

There are people on the bus, seven people plus Gilly and the driver. The people appear to be socially distanced. The driver wears a mask.

Behind the driver sits a middle-aged woman with two large sacks and no mask.

Across the aisle and three rows back sits a young man with a backpack and a mask.

Four rows behind him sits an older woman in a purple dress and purple mask.

Gilly sits three rows behind her and across the aisle. Masked.

Three teenaged boys without masks sit two rows behind her.

On the back row sits a man with a duffle bag, no mask.

Gilly tugs her mask higher on her cheeks.

Gilly wishes, too late, she had not touched her face.

Gilly fetches hand sanitizer from the pocket of her jeans and squirts it on her hands.

Along the route, the bus pulls off the highway to stop at gas stations and small general stores where people get off and on. The man with the backpack gets off. A woman gets on with two children, both girls, no masks. New passengers hesitate at the front of the bus to look around before settling into empty seats.

Gilly has been thinking of nice ways to say, don't you dare, if anyone tries to sit too close to her.

Gilly wants to remember what Una told her. It is hard to hold the words in her mind. Like holding water in her hands. Some words, she suspects, will be important to remember.

What were they?

Now she is thinking of Eva.

There is this thing that happens when she thinks of Eva, a sharp breath in and then it becomes difficult to breathe. Quickly it turns into a shallow fluttering breath, a shallow fluttering heartbeat, a pain in her chest as if it has been sucked dry. There is a caving in of her mind toward the pure pinpoint of a scream.

She does not scream.

On the bus, she makes herself breathe a long, slow breath in, and then a long, slow breath out. Her chest feels as if something crucial for life has been taken from her, and yet she is breathing. She wonders if she should feel guilty for breathing.

There is this other thing that happens when she thinks of Eva, like standing on the edge of a dark, hole, so deep she cannot see the bottom. Standing on the edge of the dark, bottomless hole, she senses something is behind her. Somebody. She feels it. She knows that the something or the somebody will push her into the hole but she does not know when. It could be soon. Or not. Sometimes she tries to pick out which is more terrifying, the hole or the not knowing.

Now, on this bus, for the first time since Eva's death, she does not feel panicked by the hole or the not knowing. She does not feel panic. She wonders why.

She wonders if it is the box.

Gilly does not know how the box works.

She suspects this is also a test.

To believe it works without knowing how.

The sun streaming through the window of the bus is warm. The wheels on the bus hum as they roll along the asphalt. A droning. Like music.

Gilly remembers.

A documentary on drone music. Rather, a composer of drone music who lived just outside the radiant city. Gilly was the one who had financed the documentary, a beloved project that a producer had wanted to make for a very long time, only,

no money.

Gilly was the money.

The one who saved the day.

Those were days when a producer could spread out into the world.

The producer sent out a camera crew to bring back footage of lakes and forests and coastlines, meadows and mountaintops. Images of isolation to accompany the spare and isolating music.

Gilly wonders if the time of isolation as comfort has passed.

Gilly remembers.

On first listen she found the droning music unlistenable. Then, over the weeks and months of listening, something changed. It seemed to change in a single moment. There was a *before*, when the music was unlistenable, then an *after*, when the music made sense. It became beautiful, this music.

In a single moment the music moved from unbearable to irresistible.

She remembers, once she played it for Eva.

Who said, turn off that crap.

Eva never had time to reach the moment when the music became irresistible.

Gilly wedges her jacket between the window and the seatback. She leans her head against the jacket.

She closes her eyes. Lulled by the sun and the droning and the disquieting memories, she falls asleep.

The box is gone.

Gilly is jolted awake by the bus lurching back onto the highway. She looks out the window and sees that the bus had stopped in front of a bank, here in a small town set down in the fields and forests far from the radiant city. Three blocks of a Main Street form the town's center. Diagonal parking spaces abut the sidewalks.

Her hands are the first to sense the absence. She looks down at her lap.

She screams.

She bends down, looks underneath her seat, underneath the seat in front of her. She stands up. Frantically she scans the bus. Gone are the teenagers, the woman in purple, the woman with the sacks, and the man with the duffle.

Wait! Stop!

Gilly presses her face against the window to see if she can see who took her box, but there is no one. No teenagers, no woman in purple, no woman with sacks, no man with duffle.

The sidewalks are empty.

The streets are empty.

The porches, the yards, the parking lots they pass as the bus rolls down the street out of town. All are empty. As if all the people evaporated.

The bus driver will not stop the bus.

Gilly walks up and down the aisle asking every passenger, did you see my box? Did you see who took it?

People flinch. They draw away from her. They shake their heads and avert their eyes.

No one saw her box. No one knows what she is talking about.

If they know, they aren't talking.

Gilly cannot stay on this bus.

Gilly is beset by a shallow fluttering breath, a shallow fluttering heartbeat, a pain in her chest as if it has been sucked dry. She feels a caving in of her mind toward the pure pinpoint of a scream. She screams.

She makes the driver stop.

She jumps off the bus.

She stands in the grass by the side of the road.

She leans over, hands on knees, sucks in shallow breaths and watches the back of the bus grow smaller and smaller and smaller and smaller and smaller until she cannot see it.

She closes her eyes.

What a fuck-up.

Gilly cannot believe she lost that damn box. She can't believe it. How hard can it be to take care of a box?

Not hard.

How easy was it to fuck it up?

Too easy. She is the fuck-up, the royal fuck-up, and there is no recovering.

What's she supposed to do now?

How's she supposed to live now?

Now.

A new thought all of a sudden, unbidden, not entirely welcome.

It is hard, near impossible, to be a human and not fuck up.

Is this true?

She looks around.

Gilly is standing next to a field planted with something. Soybeans, maybe. She does not know the name of the plant covering this big field.

Across the highway, another field, and in the distance, cows. Beyond the cows is a small yellow frame house and then a larger barn in a shade of gray brown.

Or maybe brown gray.

Gilly hears the wind. She hears birdsong. She looks down the highway toward the town. She cannot see the town from here, but it can't be far.

She could turn back and walk into the town and try to find the teenagers and the purple lady and the sack lady and the duffle man. She could knock on every door in that small town and demand information about her box. Gilly might, in fact, find the box.

Then what?

What will she do with the box?

How does the box work?

What's even in that box?

Does she have to possess the box for it to work?

Gilly considers the box, now that she has lost it. It is a box painted, not very well, red and blue and purple and gold. It is latched with a cheap, tiny hook. She thinks, without wanting to think,

It isn't the box. It never was the box.

A childish belief. In a childish box.

Gilly knows a few things.

She knows she believed there were answers.

She knows she wanted to believe there was a plan. A purpose. A trick or two, maybe.

Like a test. A test that she would pass because she was good at tests.

Gilly knows she wanted to believe she had the capacity for control, that she could tame randomness, chart a path, will a future into being.

Gilly wanted to believe she had the capacity to understand more than was reasonable.

Gilly wanted to believe in magic.

Gilly wanted to believe she was different.

Gilly knows she wanted to believe, that which was owed her, she had earned.

Gilly sits down in the grass. She makes herself breathe one slow breath and then another. It is difficult to breathe. She does it anyway.

She thinks, and her head hurts from thinking.

She thinks anyway.

The box is gone.

Eva is dead.

We are in a global pandemic.

The world is unjust.

Nobody knows what's going to happen.

I don't know what's going to happen.

I know that one day I will die.

All of these things are stupid.

All of these things are true.

None of these things should be as they are.

All of these things are.

From the direction of the town, Gilly hears a new sound.

It is not the wind. It is not birdsong. It is the sound of a car coming her way.

Gilly stands up in time to stick out a timid thumb.

The car comes into view. The car speeds past without slowing. It is the first car she has seen since the bus disappeared on the long highway.

Gilly understands, there aren't going to be a lot of cars on this road.

Gilly understands, in a global pandemic, nobody is going to pick her up.

She pulls out her phone.

BOOK XIII

Gilly says, I'll wear a mask, I swear to god.

I will ride on the top of your car, if you want. I do not have this virus, I am certain, I am sure, but whatever it takes. I'll ride with my head sticking out of the window. I'll fucking ride in the trunk, if you'll just come get me out of here.

Gilly says, I don't know who else to call.

Lawrence drives a silver Lexus hybrid.

It takes three-and-a-half-hours to reach her.

Gilly waits in the shade of a grove of pin oaks she ran into, walking back toward the small town where there may or may not be a person who is holding her box. She has finished all the water she brought with her. She is hungry and thirsty. Her hair is long and tangled. She is hollow-faced and tired. She breathes shallow breaths, waiting.

The silver car emerges from the horizon. Above, the sky has turned white-gray with the lowering sun. The car comes down the steamy, straight, and gray-black highway.

Gilly stands up.

Gilly puts on a mask.

Lawrence slows the car. He makes a U-turn and stops in front of Gilly.

Lawrence puts on a mask.

Gilly gets in.

Lawrence heads back toward the radiant city.

Lawrence is surprised to see Gilly without a silk suit.

He recognizes the red tee shirt with the black fist that Eva used to wear.

He is surprised to see Gilly in the shirt. He is surprised to see it so dirty. He does not mention it.

212 - CATHERINE LANDIS

Gilly says, I miss her.

Lawrence says, she deserves to be missed. There is a hole in the universe where she used to be, he says.

Gilly nods. She feels the tears and cannot stop them. She turns toward the window and wipes the tears from her eyes. She pulls down her mask and wipes her nose on the sleeve of the red tee shirt. She wonders whether tears carry viruses.

Lawrence points to the hand sanitizer in the cup holder.

Lawrence says, you did good work, the two of you. Never forget that. Eva will be remembered and so will you. It was important work. It was not nothing.

Gilly shakes her head. She says, it was all Eva.

Eva the creator.

Gilly the destroyer.

Lawrence is surprised. He has never heard Gilly disparage herself.

Lawrence says, we are, all of us, some of both.

I really am sorry about that vase, Lawrence, Gilly says.

Lawrence nods. He says, it was just a vase.

Lawrence has not been to the Station since the pandemic began. He has hardly been out of his house.

But he has been working.

Projects have not been abandoned. Lawrence has found ways to keep them going.

Lawrence says, you might be happy to hear, our writers are busy. Our producers, assistant producers, graphic designers; I've so far laid off no one. Not one person. Let me put it this way, nobody working for me has time to bake bread.

The work is digital, he explains. The work is through Zoom, but it's work. The virus has not stopped the work.

Lawrence catches Gilly up, brings her up to speed, tells her what she'll need to know when she is ready to come back to work.

There is something in his voice. What is it that Gilly hears?

Excitement?

Gilly has not heard excitement in a voice since Eva died.

Gilly has not heard excitement in a voice since the pandemic began.

And what of her own voice? Has it lost the timbre of excitement? She wonders.

Gilly does not know what to say.

Gilly remembers a time when she would have been jealous of Lawrence.

That time feels like a long, long, long time ago.

It was not that long ago.

Gilly remembers a time when she would not have thought Lawrence had it in him.

Gilly remembers a time when she was the one. The indispensable one.

The only indispensable one.

Gilly does not feel jealous.

She feels grateful.

Close to his heart, Lawrence has kept one project.

It is the story about two brothers who lost their land through the treachery of a system designed to take their land. One of the two brothers was his father. It is an old family story.

The boss of people with ideas, Lawrence has been patient.

He has never spoken of this story.

He has been particularly resistant to telling his story to Gilly.

Gilly is beautiful. Gilly is confident. Gilly can be ruthless. When Gilly walks in a room, people say, wait a minute. People say who is that? When Gilly puts her hand on your arm and looks at you in the eye you forget what you are thinking. Your mind is scrambled.

Lawrence's mind is not scrambled. But he is careful with his heart.

What if Gilly laughs.

One hour passes.

Lawrence begins to realize that Gilly is not speaking.

He is speaking.

Gilly is listening.

He looks over at her to see if she has fallen asleep.

No.

She is listening.

Lawrence is not sure who this Gilly is.

A Gilly in a red shirt with a black fist. A Gilly who listens. A Gilly who disparages herself.

You are not speaking, he says.

I don't have anything to say, she says.

Lawrence talks because Gilly is not talking.

He talks to keep himself awake.

He talks because he does not know if he will get this chance again.

Lawrence tells Gilly the story of the two brothers and the land.

He tells Gilly how he would make a film about the brothers and the land that was taken.

He talks away the miles and the hours.

He talks until he runs out of things to say.

Gilly does not laugh.

Gilly is thinking about how she might help Lawrence make the film about the brothers and the land that was taken. She is thinking about how to make the film about the brother in prison for a crime he did not commit.

Gilly is thinking but she is not speaking.

She does not yet know what to say.

There is silence under the starlit sky.

Silence swells the starlit sky.

After many hours, they can make out the glow of the lights from the radiant city.

The lights rise to meet the starlit sky.

When they reach the radiant city, Gilly asks Lawrence to take her to the Station.

In front of the station, Lawrence stops the car. He says, What do you want to do?

Gilly says, What do you want to do?

Lawrence looks to see if she's kidding.

She is not.

BOOK XIV

Down the halls of the Station Gilly walks in sneakers with no socks. The halls are dark. Lights from the radiant city shine through the windows.

Gilly walks past the open doors of the cluttered offices where once huddled producers, and assistant producers, and writers, and camera operators and sound and photography and make up and graphic design.

Gilly misses the chatter, from the complainers and the creators, both.

Gilly understands, there was a lot to complain about.

Gilly finds the double doors that lead into the studio where there is a small desk and a chair built for her by a craftsman she found in Southern Virginia. It is dark. She sits down on the floor.

Lawrence finds her sitting on the floor.

Gilly says, these stories cannot wait.

Lawrence says, there's a Zoom meeting at 8 in the morning.

Gilly says, I'll be there. If you need me.

Lawrence says, We need everybody.

Gilly says, we have a lot of work to do.

Let's begin.

Epilogue

After the plague, the women are walking.

No masks.

The mask years are over. The women walk along paths in the new park just outside the radiant city. They are new paths.

Woven between shade trees and gardens and fountains and memorials for the dead.

Gilly is older now.

She is surprised to have a friend

To walk with along the paths between the memorials for the dead.

She had thought she could not have another friend

After Eva.

But here she is.

"It's the oldest story in the world," Gilly says to her new friend.

"What is? You mean love?"

"No."

"Sex, then."

"No."

"Money?"

"No."

"Treachery? Betrayal, envy, hubris, greed, is that it? Greed? Truth, beauty, desire, or what's that, not empathy exactly, but..."

"No."

"Compassion, is it compassion?"

"Death. It's death."

"Oh, that."

Gilly says, can I tell you a story?

Acknowledgments

Thanks go to the teachers who nurtured my love of literature and also of mythology, and who encouraged my writing at pivotal points. Namely, the late Carol Stein at Girls Preparatory School, and, at Davidson College, Dr. Gill Holland, the late Dr. Tony Abbott, and Dr. Charlie Cornwell. I have read several versions of the *Epic of Gilgamesh* over the years, but Stephen Mitchell's GILGAMESH, Free Press, 2004, was the one I relied on most to guide me while writing *Gilly and Eva*.

A PLAGUE OF GODS had its readers, for whom I am grateful for their guidance and support. Mary Smith, Lettie Flores, Chelsea Bauer, Shiela Wood-Navaro, Christy Mabe Scott, and Steve Peeples.

Mostly I give credit and thanks to my sons, Bruce and Charlie, who were the first to read my quirky version of *Gilgamesh*, and whose enthusiastic affirmation spurred me to write the rest of the stories.

I am ever mindful of the support, both emotional and material, of my husband. As always, thank you, Bruce.

Catherine Landis is the author of a memoir, TWO TRAINS LEAVE THE STATION: *A Meditation on Aging, Alzheimer's, and Arithmetic,* and two novels, SOME DAYS THERE'S PIE and HARVEST. She is the mother of two grown sons and the grandmother of two grandsons. She is a runner, hiker, activist for progressive causes, and a pretty good cook. She lives in Knoxville Tennessee with her husband.

CPSIA information can be obtained
at www.ICGtesting.com
Printed in the USA
LVHW020524051022
729981LV00003B/7